"You don't shape up to the star billing."

Ben ignored Kate's gasp of astonishment and went on. "I'd never have thought your father could be so blinded by paternal emotions."

Kate's mind whirled. What had her father said about her to this rude, arrogant partner of his? "I resent what you've been saying, Mr. High-and-Mighty Ben Croft, because you don't know anything about it!"

His reply began on a sneer. "I know what I see and I've seen nothing of the calm, self-assured rational woman I was given to expect," he said. "Are you trying to tell me there's a real woman under that facade?"

Before Kate could reply his lips were on hers, his right arm cradling her into the hardness of his chest as he kissed her expertly, endlessly....

Stag at Bay

Victoria Gordon

Harlequin Books

TORONTO • NEW YORK • LONDON
AMSTERDAM • PARIS • SYDNEY • HAMBURG
STOCKHOLM • ATHENS • TOKYO • MILAN

Original hardcover edition published in 1982
by Mills & Boon Limited

ISBN 0-373-02690-0

Harlequin Romance first edition May 1985

CHAPTER ONE

A JAGGED spear of too-close lightning flashed down from a sky filled with roiling black clouds, briefly revealing the gateway before surrendering the eerie sight to the inky, rain-soaked shroud of night.

Kate jammed her foot on the brake, her eyes unfocussed by the sudden brilliance and the unexpected vision of the high gateway that was still beyond the range of her headlights. The small car slithered and skittered on the soggy gravel, coming finally to a halt as another lightning bolt seared earthward amidst the booming thunder of the first.

Again the gate was illuminated, and Kate's earlier impression was shiveringly confirmed. On the high white crossbar of the gateway, fully twenty feet above the ground, the weather-bleached skull of a massively-antlered stag glared down at her through vacant eye-sockets given an unholy life by the lightning.

She shivered again as a wave of thunder rumbled out of the turbulent sky and more lightning, farther away this time, flared through the driving curtain of rain.

Slowly, carefully, she inched the car closer, until finally the headlights revealed the sign on the massive wire gates: KATHRYN DOWNS.

She sighed with partial relief; at last she'd found the place. It had been the weather, more than her father's mapmaking, which had made her so much later than expected.

Chewing idly on her lower lip, she sat staring into the maelstrom of thunder, lightning and sheets of rain. She

5

had absolutely no desire to go out into *that*, and she muttered a gentle curse on whoever had decided to shut the high wire structure against her. Then she glanced down at her pale, light linen suit and flimsy, high-heeled shoes and mouthed a stronger curse—this time at herself. Certainly it was no one else's fault that she'd chosen to wear such totally inappropriate clothing for the final leg of her journey.

Lightning flashed again, too close for comfort this time, and she peered upward at the looming skull, silently imploring the ghastly figure to do something. Open the gate, or stop the rain . . . anything!

It was little consolation to know that her suitcase, on the rear seat of the car, held a welter of clothing that was at least reasonably suitable for a journey into the high hinterland of Queensland's Sunshine Coast. Before leaving Melbourne she had wisely purchased several pairs of blue jeans, some light shirts, even a pair of stout walking shoes. And she had even worn them during the first four days of her long, almost two-thousand-kilometre journey through Wagga Wagga, Dubbo, Moree and Warwick to reach Brisbane late the evening before.

But in Brisbane that morning, with sunny skies giving no suggestion of the weather to come, she had decided to dress up properly for the final drive, the drive that would see her being welcomed by the loving father she had not seen in two long years.

And now this. 'Damn,' Kate muttered to herself. 'Damn and double damn!' Even to step from the car would mean writing off her favourite suit, and for all her planning she had neither umbrella nor raincoat. She looked again at the curtain of rain, then sighed her despair and turned to clamber into the back seat.

Getting out of the suit was easy enough despite the

cramped conditions, but the struggle she had to wriggle into the tight jeans, still stiff with newness, made her giggle at the whole ridiculousness of the situation.

She was still giggling happily, her head buried in the folds of the T-shirt she was pulling over her mane of straw-berry-blonde hair, when a flare of exceptionally strong lightning blazed squarely into her eyes through the thin fabric of the garment.

Lightning? Realisation struck her as she yanked down the T-shirt and found herself blinded by the beam of a powerful torch. Blinded, but not deafened. Even through the closed car window and the drum of rain on the roof, she heard clearly the explosive words from outside.

'What the hell . . .?' The voice died and Kate's instincts leaped to her defence. Her fingers slammed down on the door lock even as she felt a tug from outside the car.

Then fresh lightning glowed from the sky and the figure outside the car turned to look upward, momentarily lowering the torch. Kate shuddered. In the brief flash she saw only a grotesque, towering figure, shapeless beneath a rain-blackened cloak.

'Get away. Oh, please, get away,' she whispered aloud in a terror that turned her bones to water. Where an instant before she had contemplated leaping somehow into the front seat, where at least she might be able to drive away from this horror, now she could only whimper in stark fear.

The torch beam flashed into her eyes once again, but only fleetingly. Then it was turned back on the figure holding it, angled so that Kate was no longer blinded. What she saw was small comfort—a battered, dripping Western-style hat, an oilskin slicker, and between them, a face that seemed designed to frighten children.

It was all planes and angles, a thin, high-bridged hawk's

nose, prominent cheekbones, a slit of a mouth and a strong,
deeply-cleft chin. And the eyes—deeply hooded and
gleaming like emeralds from beneath the brim of the hat.
There was strength there, a fearsome strength. Like
something carved from rock, until suddenly the mouth
quirked into a wry grin and the head shook lightly from
side to side.

Still holding the torch on himself, the man pantomimed
a series of gestures directing Kate to lower the window
between them.

In her stunned silence, only the negative shaking of her
head could reply, and his grin began to fade. Then, surprisingly, he stepped back a few paces, still holding the
light so she could see his face. Gingerly, Kate lowered the
window a scant two inches, keeping her fingers ready to
close it again.

The voice that boomed from the dripping spectre seemed
loud as the thunder.

'You'll be Kate Lester, I presume, but could I ask just
what in *hell* you were doing?'

'Lyle,' she replied automatically. 'Kate Lyle.' Not Kate
Lester . . . not ever again, but the transition to her maiden
name required constant reminders from within.

'That tells me a lot,' he replied, stepping one pace closer
and then withdrawing instantly as Kate hastily yanked on
the window lever.

'What's the matter with you?' he shouted against the
roar of wind and rain and thunder. He seemed genuinely
surprised that Kate should fear him, despite having stepped
from the storm-racked night like a grim phantom.

'It should be obvious enough, you . . . Peeping Tom!'
she cried, anger for the first time beginning to override her
terror.

Strong white teeth gleamed in the torch beam as he

threw back his head in throaty laughter that echoed through the confines of the car.

'Peeping Tom? I can assure you, dear child, that I'm sufficiently conversant with the female form to have no need to play ridiculous games like that on a night like this.'

'Well then, just what were you doing?' Kate demanded.

His laugh ended, mouth shut like a trap before he sneered out a reply. 'Mostly I've been standing out in the rain holding the gate open while you did your little strip-tease in the back seat,' he replied.

Strip-tease! 'I was not!' Kate squealed angrily. 'I was merely . . .'

'Playing Superman, only there wasn't a phone booth handy,' he jeered, interrupting her. 'Just too bad you didn't open your eyes; you'd be home and dry by now without the quick change.'

'Well, thank you very much,' she retorted. 'And you might have let me know you were there, instead of sneaking around like some kind of . . . of . . .'

'Oh, try *pervert*,' he snarled. 'My God, but you're an ungrateful wench—and paranoid, to boot, from the sound of things! Well, I've got better things to do than trade insults in this weather. Now that you've got your clothes on, why don't you see if you can manage to find the house by yourself and get some coffee on? I'll be along once I've locked up.'

And without waiting for Kate to reply, he turned on his heel and stalked away into the darkness, heading for the gate. Kate muttered an angry reply and floundered her way into the front seat. She started the car and flipped on the headlights to reveal the dripping intruder standing impatiently by the open gates.

As she surged the car forward, he bowed in a sarcastic gesture that quickly turned to outrage as she deliberately steered through a puddle and thoroughly drenched him as she passed. A convenient lightning flash showed him shaking an angry fist as she sped down the slippery track.

Her father's letters had only partially prepared Kate for the house that loomed into view as she dipped over the first ridge past the high gateway. She had known it was a fairly typical Queensland colonial home, with spreading verandahs on each side and a curiously-sloped roof of corrugated iron, but he hadn't revealed the immensity of the building. As Kate drove up as close as she could to the main entry, the structure reared high above her, massive in the glow of the yard lights.

Ahead of her was a series of iron-roofed outbuildings, slightly to the left a barn that seemed even larger than the house, and farther on yet a structure that seemed to be a corral with loading chutes and raceways, only it was totally boarded in, and adjoined a series of high-fenced yards and small paddocks.

Leaving her gear in the car, Kate made a mad dash for the shelter of the verandah, getting soaked even in the few steps required for the journey. She ran fingers through her tangle of long hair, then dismissed her appearance with a shrug and stepped forward to knock loudly on the front door.

'Dad? Are you there?' No answer. She called again, then tried the door and wasn't overly surprised to find it open. But where was her father? Surely the hired man she'd encountered at the gate wouldn't have sent her along if Henry Lyle wasn't on the property . . . or would he? The tall stranger had known who Kate was, obviously expected her, but would a hired man have the temerity to demand that the owner's daughter make him coffee? Something didn't ring quite true.

It took Kate several minutes to scurry through the im-

mense house, peering into empty room after empty room
in a vain search that finally ended in the huge lounge
room beside the front entry. There, at least, she found
evidence that her father had actually been in this house.
His second-favourite pipe lay in a holder beside a large
armchair and sections of the one wall-to-wall bookcase
held volumes she knew.

But where could he be? Suddenly chilled from the
dampness of her clothes, Kate shivered. Or was it from the
damp? The huge house, which had looked so welcoming
from the storm outside, now took on an ominous atmosphere by its very emptiness.

A window rattled in the wind; rain smashed like surf on
the iron roof, and from the rear of the house came an
irregular, inexplicable creaking—and then a crashing
sound that made Kate leap with alarm.

'That coffee ready yet?' She spun around to see a shadowy figure emerge ghostlike from a doorway she hadn't
known about. The voice identified him clearly enough,
but without his hat and bulky slicker he loomed even taller
than she remembered.

A khaki shirt and trousers testified to the slicker's in-
efficiency, and the man's dark brown hair was curled into
tiny waves from the dampness. Even his socks were soaked,
Kate noticed as he moved catlike towards her, leaving
damp patches wherever he stepped.

'Well?' His voice held a note of impatience, and once his
eyes had met Kate's, he no longer bothered to wait for an
answer.

Contempt—or was it merely anger?—flashed in his deep
green eyes, and he shook his head wearily as he turned to
stalk away from her, obviously heading for the kitchen.
Kate, following, almost had to run to keep up.

'Hey! Stop, damn it!' she cried. 'Where's my father?'

As well cry at the wind; the tall man ignored her as he stepped into the kitchen and began rummaging through the routine of coffee making.

'You answer me,' Kate shouted. 'Where is my father? Where is he?' Then she was repeating that final question over and over and over as panic stole control of her mouth. She was immediately behind the man, drumming on his impassive shoulders with futile blows and hardly aware of what she was saying or doing.

He turned, then, and hands like claws gripped her by the shoulders, lifting her clear of the floor as he shook her like a puppy. The shaking was so severe that her neck flopped loosely and her panting breath left no strength to continue her harangue.

'Settle down!' The order slammed into her consciousness as the man forcibly plunked her on the floor with a jarring thud.

'Now,' he said, eyes burning into her own as he demanded her attention, 'I'll tell you all about your father. But right at this moment I'm tired and hungry and— thanks to you—wetter than I need to be or want to be. So I'm going to put on some dry clothes; then we'll talk.'

He paused momentarily as if to assure himself she was still listening, then continued. 'And you're going to sit there, quietly, and watch that coffee pot. And when it's ready you're going to pour us each a cup. Mine will be white with two sugars. I strongly suggest a drop of brandy for both of us . . . there's some in that sideboard over there. Now is that all perfectly clear, Mrs Lester?' And, with astonishing gentleness, he eased Kate into a kitchen chair and walked out of the room without waiting for any answer.

Shaken by the confusion and the unexpected harshness of the encounter, Kate slumped in the chair, trembling and afraid. She could feel the imprint of his fingers on her shoulders, and the burning intensity of his green eyes seemed to remain in the room after his departure.

She was still sitting there, dazed, when he returned a few minutes later, dressed in clean khaki and with his dark hair combed into a semblance of order.

He stood over her for a moment, a massive, vibrant figure that wore a tangible aura of vitality. Then he turned away with a curious shake of his head and poured each of them a cup of the coffee, adding a generous dollop of brandy before asking Kate her preferences about sugar and cream.

'Black . . . thanks,' she murmured, forcing herself not to flinch as he reached close to put the cup down in front of her. He took his own coffee and seated himself across the table from her, as if somehow sensing that his very nearness was frightening to her.

He sipped slowly at his coffee, using his eyes in a silent demand that Kate follow suit, and not until her cup was half empty did he speak, this time with unexpected gentleness.

'Now, let's start all over and see if we can get off on the right foot this time,' he said with a hint of a friendly grin. 'First, I suppose, introductions. I'm Ben Croft. I'm your father's partner, as I imagine you know. I'm not a rapist or a bogey-man, or even a Peeping Tom. And I mean you no harm whatsoever, despite the fact that you nearly ran over my foot out there by the gate and you did it deliberately.'

He grinned, this time a broad, generous smile that revealed strong, even teeth and made pleasant little wrinkles around his eyes. 'And I'm sorry I shook you up as I did, but you were getting just a bit hysterical. Which,' and his smile broadened, 'is probably fair enough, now that I think about it. Certainly not the welcome you expected, anyway.'

Kate said nothing, but her eyes never left his face. The warmth of the brandy and coffee was settling her nerves quickly, and her mind was occupied in sorting out what he'd said.

Of course! Benton Croft. But hardly the man she'd expected him to be. Her father's letters had sung his praises to the skies, but had implied a suave—urbane businessman. Not, for whatever reason, the ruffian at the gate or even this much gentler version. The Benton Croft she'd visualised was a jet-setter, a one-man business empire with tentacles in several countries. A money man.

'You're not exactly what I expected, either,' he said softly, and Kate's eyes widened with alarm. God! Was he reading her mind?

'I ... I don't know what you mean,' she stammered. And then, more strongly, 'What about my father?'

She might as well not have spoken. Ben Croft continued, almost musingly, holding her with his eyes as he spoke.

'You're too thin; you've got terrible smudges under your eyes; and you're spooky, running on your nerves ... probably have been since ... looks like you haven't had a decent meal since then, either. Feed you up a bit ... probably as stubborn as your ... just hope you'll be able to ...' The words fluttered around her like butterflies, touching her consciousness but not penetrating.

The brandy rolled in her stomach and for a second she feared she would faint. Then Ben Croft's words forced themselves into her mind and she reared upright in alarm.

'Your father's all right, but he's in hospital. I took him in yesterday. Now, hold on! There's no sense getting excited,' he cautioned, reaching out across the table to grip Kate's wrist and stop her from leaping to her feet.

brandy into a clean glass and steadied Kate's hand while she slurped it down.

'You'll be right in a moment,' he said, then glanced at his wristwatch. 'And since I gather you now agree with me about not rushing off to the hospital, I'll just phone and square things away for tomorrow.'

Kate's only reply was a vague nod, but she sat and listened as he telephoned the hospital in Nambour and finally got through to whoever was in charge that evening.

'. . . just a message,' he said. 'When it's convenient I should like Mr Henry Lyle to be informed that his daughter has arrived safely, and that we'll be in to collect him tomorrow morning.'

The call completed, he turned his attention once again to Kate, his voice immediately switching from firm authority to a gentle, comforting murmur.

'And for you, I think, a good night's sleep is in order. How long since you've eaten, by the way? Today? Yesterday? Or do you even remember?'

'I had something this morning,' Kate replied, not really interested enough to tell him that the *something* had been only a cup of coffee en route through Brisbane.

'Well then, I think a decent meal is in order,' Ben Croft mused, half to himself. 'No, you sit still and work on the rest of that brandy. I'm housebroken well enough to feed both of us without poisoning anybody.'

And Kate sat there, silent and lost in her own thoughts, as he bustled about the kitchen with complete confidence, breaking eggs, grilling thick slabs of steak and slicing onion, tomatoes and lettuce for a simple salad.

Kate wasn't at all hungry. She hadn't, it seemed, been hungry for . . . how long? Since Wayne's accident, anyway. Since the police had arrived to tell her about it, to tell her *all* about it, in a degree of detail that flourished and spread until it emerged full-blown at the inquest. The inquest that still sometimes featured in Technicolor nightmares as Wayne's questionable reputation and Kate's own illusions—what few remained after sixteen months of marriage—fell in tatters and dissolved.

What hadn't come out at the inquest, but had stayed in festering silence inside Kate herself, was her own knowledge of her so-called husband's illicit activities. She had *known* where he was that fateful night. Not exactly *where*, of course, but the circumstances, the dreary, sordid circumstances.

She had known, in fact, almost from the beginning of their marriage that Wayne was a gambler, a lecher and an incorrigible womaniser. Known it, and by her own inaction, condoned it. Until that very night, the night he had finally taken one drink too many in the company of his latest conquest, then gone out to drive on the crowded Saturday night streets and fulfil Kate's heartfelt wish.

The policeman who had brought her the tale had interpreted her wide-eyed, shivering reaction as simple shock, not knowing that she had spent the entire evening sitting in their small, messy flat, sitting in the dark and *wishing* her husband dead!

All evening . . . until the uniformed figure had arrived at her door like some monstrous fairy godfather, a harbinger of wishes fulfilled—and guilt begun.

No matter that she hadn't loved Wayne any longer, if indeed she had ever loved him. In retrospect she saw only a childish infatuation with his good looks and superficial charm, but surely there must have been love? At least in the beginning.

Kate's guilt was ludicrous; intellectually she knew it herself. Intellectually, everything took on a new and quite different perspective, like this tall man who was busy cooking a meal for her—after being insulted and threatened and not even knowing her in the first place. Wayne, handsome, selfish Wayne, wouldn't have cooked for her on her deathbed; it simply wouldn't have occurred to him to involve himself in women's work.

With both of them working, and Kate's job at the university had been, she often suspected, the most demanding because of the overtime, she had tried occasionally to interest him in sharing the household tasks. To a stock reply:

'If I'd wanted to wash dishes (or clean the oven, or help with the ironing, or take out the trash, or . . .) I wouldn't have bothered getting married.' They hadn't been married long before Kate stopped asking.

'Hey! I asked how you like your steak?' Ben Croft's gentle voice intruded, but not so harshly that it startled her. She came back to reality slowly, but without fear, and for the first time she smiled at him.

'Whatever's easiest,' she replied. 'So long as it doesn't moo and jump off the plate.'

'Not likely!' he replied with feigned outrage. 'This is venison steak, young lady, and you can have it any way you like so long as it's medium rare. Well, maybe medium.'

'You're the chef,' Kate replied. Venison! Not so very surprising, perhaps, considering this man and her father were partners in a deer farm. But still rather unexpected. She'd never tasted venison.

And for the first time in months, hunger—actual, raw, stomach-growling hunger—reared up and demanded a place in Kate's attentions. And all of her senses responded, newly wakened like spring flowers. She smelled the heady, slightly liverish odour of searing venison steak, the various spices he'd added, the tang of the onion. It was . . . heavenly.

The meal, placed before her a moment later, looked tantalising, a judicious mingling of colours and textures. Kate's ears perked up to the sound of a wine bottle opening, and a ruby-red claret appeared on the table between them.

'Should have let it breathe a bit, I suppose, but I forgot,' Ben Croft muttered, with no real hint of apology in his flashing grin.

To Kate, it couldn't have mattered less; she reacted to the sight of the food like one of Pavlov's dogs. Neither of them spoke, then, until some time later, when Ben's plate was empty and Kate was struggling to finish her own huge meal. Whereupon she only barely managed to subdue a combination of hiccup and burp as she leaned back in her seat, more genuinely comfortable than she could ever remember.

'You're truly wasted in business, Mr Croft,' she sighed. 'You should be chained up in the kitchen of some very posh restaurant.'

'It's Ben ... Kate,' he replied gently. 'And I've got better things to do with my time than play chef to the world. I only cook for myself ... and my friends.'

'Well, you could certainly give me lessons,' she replied.

'Perhaps one day I will, although I remember Henry saying rather often that you're an excellent cook.'

'I ... haven't had much chance ... lately,' she replied rather lamely. Not much of an explanation, but easier than trying to explain how Wayne's destruction of her had extended even to creating doubt about things she knew she did well.

'No, I suppose not,' Ben replied thoughtfully. For a moment he looked like continuing, but whatever else he might have said was halted by a yawn Kate didn't know was coming.

'I think it's bedtime for you,' said Ben. 'Come and I'll show you your room. You could probably do with a hot shower while I bring in your gear.'

'Oh, but . . . the dishes!' she protested, only to have him shrug away the problem as a minor annoyance.

'I'll do them later, or they can wait until morning for all the difference it makes. If you're as tired as you look you'd only be dropping them anyway.'

Kate followed him up the wide staircase, which was almost blocked by the width of his shoulders, and to the doorway of a high-ceilinged bedroom, where Ben halted. 'Shower's through there,' he said with a gesture towards the other side of the room. 'See that you don't go to sleep in there; I've been as wet today as I want to be.'

He flashed her a deliberately wicked grin and loped down the stairs without waiting for a reply. When she peeped from the steamy en suite bathroom some time later, all her cases were neatly stacked by the bed and her linen suit was tidily hung up in the closet.

Dry and warm in her nightgown, Kate lay down on the wide double bed with no expectation of sleeping. She was incredibly revitalised from the shower, she thought, closing her eyes for a minute. She opened them again to slanting beams of strong sunlight, halfway between dawn and midday.

'My God!' she cried, flinging off the coverlet and running over to stare out the window. Memory caught up with her halfway there, and with it a vague confusion of half-formed images in her mind.

Surely she'd lain down on top of the coverlet? And surely the window had been closed, last night, against the wind-driven rain? Yet she had wakened beneath the coverlet, and the window now was open to the morning breeze. And why this fleeting, delicate memory of being tucked in, of being gently kissed on the forehead as the cover was snugged round her shoulders?

There could be only one obvious explanation, she had to admit as she rushed through her toilet and then, less quickly, moved down the wide stairway and into the huge kitchen.

She found, to her great relief, that the kitchen was empty, the only sign of life the electric percolator bubbling gently away to itself. She sighed gratefully at the chance to think through a cup of coffee before the inevitable meeting with Ben Croft, that strange, moody giant who could shake her silly one minute and tuck her in like a child the next.

An unusual, vibrant man, strangely unsettling even now that her original fears were proved ridiculous. And yet, she knew, Ben Croft was a dangerous man, a man not to be crossed or trifled with. Not that she had any such intentions. She'd had a man in her life, and that was three too many. In sixteen months of marriage she had gone from an incredibly young twenty-four to a much older, very much wiser twenty-six.

Not that she could compare Ben Croft with Wayne. Not with any degree of fairness. Her every instinct told her that Ben was a very much different type indeed. Married or not, she somehow couldn't imagine him chasing after . . .

Kate shivered as her mind slipped back to the inquest, and focussed on the sluttish, vacant-eyed creature who was called to testify about Wayne's last few hours alive. She couldn't have been more than nineteen, and everything about her fairly shrieked out a blatant, animal sexuality so crude, so smugly, ignorantly, arrogantly piggish that even the sight of her had made Kate want to throw up.

Enough to try and accept her husband's womanising— but this? To have to sit in that impersonal courtroom and know that she was being compared to this . . . this *animal*.

And that everyone making the comparison would be wondering what was wrong with her, what failure in her as a woman would drive her husband to such sordid solace?

How much more amused they would have been to know that Kate had not only, obviously, failed in her role as wife and lover, but that she had coldly been wishing her husband dead at the very moment he had died!

The sound of footsteps brought her back to reality, and she looked up through tear-dimmed eyes to find Ben Croft standing in the doorway, a smile of welcome fading like smoke to be replaced by a cold, speculative, almost predatory gaze.

He smiled, then, but it was merely a gesture to convention. There was no warmth in it, nor in his voice as he spoke. It was as if he had somehow tuned himself out, creating a deliberate barrier between them.

'Unless you think breakfast is vital, I reckon we should get changed and be on our way,' he said, without so much as a 'good morning' before it. 'We can stop for a nice lunch once we've picked up your father; he'll probably be glad of a change from hospital tucker.'

He waited only long enough for Kate's acquiescence, then strode off again, presumably to his own quarters. Kate gulped down her coffee and fled upstairs, confused and more than a little piqued by his brusqueness.

She returned promptly in her linen suit, and stopped in astonishment on the stairs when Ben stepped into the foyer below.

This, she thought, was more like the Benton Croft she had imagined. Freshly shaven and dressed in what had to be a custom tailored suit of light wool, wearing expensive leather casuals and a dark tie to match the pin-stripe in his shirt, Ben looked every inch the suave, urbane businessman. Only the richness of his tan gave away his obvious penchant for outdoor work.

'That's a bit spiffy for a hospital visit, isn't it?' she quipped in an ill-timed attempt at humour. 'Dad'll think we've come to bury him or something!'

'Your sense of humour is appalling,' Ben replied curtly, standing aside to hold the door for her. Parked outside the house was a large Range Rover, and he also held the door of that while Kate clambered into the passenger seat.

He drove the vehicle skilfully, although a bit fast for her taste, considering the sloppy state of the gravel roads, but her continued attempts at conversation were bluntly stalled with monosyllabic answers.

It wasn't until they turned on to the bitumen, high on the ridge overlooking Nambour and the sea beyond, that he spoke at any length. And once he'd started, Kate wished he hadn't.

'I wasn't going to say anything, but it seems that I'll have to, in view of your father's condition,' Ben began. 'It's really his place, but knowing him I doubt if he'd make much of a job of it.'

He'd been speaking almost out of the side of his mouth, attention on his driving, but suddenly he turned and fixed his bright green eyes on Kate with an intensity that made her shiver inside.

'What I'm getting at,' he said, 'is that it's damned well high time you grew up!'

CHAPTER TWO

'I WHAT?' Kate couldn't believe she had heard him rightly.

'Grew up—as in maturity, adulthood, that sort of thing.' His eyes were once again on the road, but Kate didn't need their green highlights to accentuate the seriousness in his voice.

In the silence which followed, a silence in which she was dumbstruck with surprise and Ben seemed content to await her eventual reply, the atmosphere inside the vehicle took on a distinctly chilly tone.

She simply didn't know what to say. In her younger days, before the hell of her marriage, she would have leapt to the attack without a second thought, but now that same anger simmered under tight control.

It was Ben who finally broke the silence with a voice so soft she barely heard him.

'Gutless,' he muttered. 'Damn it, woman, aren't you even going to tell me to mind my own business? Or are you so totally screwed up you can't even manage that?'

'All right. Mind your own business,' Kate replied steadily, trembling with the need to maintain calmness.

'Not likely,' he snorted. 'I've got enough trouble keeping your old man in line without the kind of hassles you've brought along. Sorry, lady, but we're going to sort you out now, and that's all there is to it.'

'Oh, is it?' A strange, chilling calm had settled into Kate now, harbinger of an even icier anger yet to come. 'And tell me, Mr Croft, do you get some kind of sadistic little pleasures out of sorting me out? Is that how you get your kicks?'

He grinned wolfishly without taking his eyes from the steep, winding road. 'It gives me no pleasure at all, *Ms* Lyle. In fact I'd much rather not have to bother. Only with your father trying to work himself to death I had hoped you'd be a settling influence here, sort of slow the old devil down. And instead, what do I get? A weep! I'm not trying to negate your sorrow, but damn it, it's been better than three months since you were widowed and you're still running around crying in your beer as if it was yesterday. Your husband is dead, and all this feeling sorry for yourself isn't going to bring him back to life.

'But your father, I might point out, is still alive. And your father needs you—or at least he needs the girl he's so often described to me. Personally, I think he's been fooling himself.'

'And just what the hell is that supposed to mean?' Kate's voice now revealed her anger; she snapped at him like a hostile cat.

'It means you don't shape up to the star billing, sweetie,' Ben replied. 'And it rather surprises me, because I'd never have thought your dad could be quite so blinded by paternal emotions that he'd throw all judgment to the winds.'

Kate's gasp of astonishment was wasted; Ben continued without giving her a chance to speak.

'I just hope he's been better at judging our stock, but I think I'll review it myself, just in case I'm wrong.'

Kate hardly heard him. Her mind was a-whirl with horrible thoughts. What had her father said about her to this . . . this rude, arrogant partner of his? Surely he hadn't built her into some paragon, creating an impression she could never possibly live up to. He wouldn't! But then what *had* he said?

'. . . and when you deliberately held off telling him about the accident—and the funeral—until it was too late for him to get there, he thought—and I, like a fool agreed— that it was a reasonable enough approach from somebody as tough and self-reliant as he always said you were. Hell! You were probably in such a flap you never got round to thinking about him.'

'That's not true!' The words squeaked out, barely audible as Kate's throat tightened. Then she shut up. How could she possibly tell this man the real reason for her actions? And it was none of his business anyway.

'That's your story; you stick to it,' he growled in reply, suddenly swinging the vehicle off the main road and up a narrow bitumen track to the right where a layby provided parking for a scenic lookout over Nambour and the coast beyond.

He switched off the ignition with an angry flip of one powerful wrist, then turned to regard her soberly, his eyes bleak and hostile.

'The point is, now, that your father's health is more important to me than your feeling sorry for yourself. I don't care how much you loved your husband, or how much you miss him; he's gone and that's all there is to it. But unless you get your act together, and do it damn well properly, your presence here is only going to upset your father.

'So I want your promise that you'll keep your little crying jags, like that one this morning, in private. I don't care much if you cry yourself to sleep every damned night of the week—just be certain your father doesn't know about it.'

'All right!' Kate screamed back at him when he paused for a breath. 'All right! You've made your point. And let me tell you something, Mr High-and-mighty Ben Croft. I

care just as much about my father's health as you do—
probably a great deal more. And I had no intention of
moving in to become the resident cry-baby, or anything
else that would have upset Daddy. But I resent what you've
been saying, and I resent what you've obviously been
thinking, because you . . . don't . . . know . . . anything . . .
about it!'

His reply began as a sneer. 'I sure as hell know what I
see, and I've seen nothing of the calm, self-assured, rational
woman I was given to expect,' he said. 'Are you trying to
tell me there's a real woman under that façade?'

'There certainly was the last time I looked,' Kate replied
with saccharine sweetness. 'Not that I'd expect a chauvinist
like you to recognise the real thing if you saw it.'

'Chauvinist I may be, but I'm not blind,' he smiled, his
eyes roving over her slender figure with tactile sensitivity.
Kate sat, unmoving and silent, astonished at the sheer
physical reactions within her. He touched her without
touching her, and she could almost *feel* the caresses on her
throat, her lips, the swell of her breasts. Her nipples
hardened against the texture of her bra, and she silently
thanked whatever impulse had caused her to wear the bra,
which she seldom did.

'Whenever you're through, perhaps we could be on our
way,' she said, speaking slowly and distinctly to hide the
trembling inside her. Never had a man so aroused her, she
was thinking, with a growing sense of panic. It wasn't
possible, and yet this green-eyed stranger had reawakened
her long-dormant sexuality *without even touching her*.

And worse, he knew exactly what effect he was having on her. When Kate finally forced herself to meet
his eyes, having fought down an insane desire to tug her
skirt down as his eyes slowly caressed her legs, it was
only to find in them a glimmer of sardonic amusement,

a devilish, wicked joy.

'We'll go,' he said softly, 'when you've given me the promise I asked for.'

'Well then, we may sit here a long time,' Kate retorted angrily. 'For ever, even!'

'You sure don't make a lot of sense,' he replied evenly. 'You've already indicated that you agree with me, but you don't want to promise anything.'

'I don't agree with you at all,' Kate snapped. 'All I said is that I have no intention of upsetting Daddy. It has nothing whatsoever to do with your dictatorial, high-handed attitude. I don't feel I'm under any obligation to promise you anything, and I won't.'

'Okay.' He grinned wryly and leaned back against his side of the Range Rover, reaching into one pocket for his cigarettes and lighter.

Kate haughtily refused the cigarette he offered her, though she dearly wanted one, and they sat in almost agreeable silence as he smoked his own. Agreeable, in the sense that they had stopped arguing, but less comfortable for Kate because he had once again begun caressing her with his eyes, and despite her clothing she felt naked beneath his gaze.

When he finally finished the cigarette, but still made no move to start the vehicle, Kate turned on him with undisguised anger.

'I suppose we're to sit here until you get your way?' she demanded. 'Do you always expect to get your own way?'

'Usually.'

'Well, not this time. And would you stop looking at me like that?' Her own voice was pitched with frustration, while his was the essence of calm.

'Like what?'

'You know very well what I mean!'

Ben Croft's voice took on a silky smoothness, but the bold appraisal never left his eyes. 'Do I? I wonder . . .'

'Well, I don't wonder at all,' she retorted. 'Now can we stop playing silly little games and continue on to the hospital? I'm frankly more than bored with your company already, and I'd like to collect my father.'

'But you haven't promised yet.'

She could have screamed. Damn the man anyway! Damn him straight to hell. But she would *not* promise him anything, even if it meant . . .

'Right,' she muttered, grabbing at her handbag with one hand and yanking on the door handle with the other. Ben Croft merely sat, watching, and when she had swung herself halfway out, only to be arrested by the shoulder harness she had forgotten about, he laughed.

'Damn you!' she cried, twisting as she attempted to release herself. And this time he didn't laugh, but instead reached out to collect her wrist in one huge hand, yanking her back into the vehicle and across the seat towards him.

'I suppose I can't force you to promise,' he growled, 'but at least I can find out just how much woman you really think you are.'

And before Kate could protest his lips were on hers, his right arm cradling her into the hardness of his chest as he kissed her expertly, endlessly.

At first she tried to fight him, but in the solid grip of his hands she was as helpless as a child. Then she switched tactics, sagging in his arms with total submissiveness. That was even worse, as he ravished her mouth, at first hard and then more gently, his lips demanding, and getting, a reaction.

She was on fire; her breasts burning with the heat from his body and her own, the nipples hard and thrusting against him. His hand slid from her wrist to stroke her waist, her shoulder, the curve of her neck, her earlobe. And she was responding to his caress, her body betraying her needs as she instinctively strained to be closer, united with him.

Her own lips now were searching, moving to meet his and moulding themselves to his kiss. When his hand touched her thighs, they parted in expectation of his touch, ignoring the screams of protest from her mind.

Her freed hand darted down to clutch at his wrist, then abandoned all pretence and slid up the soft wool of his suit so that her fingers could tangle in his hair, pulling him closer. His lips, his touch, brought her to the brink of total submission, and then he eased her away from him.

'I don't think this is the place to continue,' he said, and Kate took remote satisfaction from the raggedness of his breath. If he had so obviously succeeded in turning her on, at least she knew he hadn't escaped unscathed himself.

'You're a . . . a proper bastard!' she gasped, yanking her other wrist free and squirming away until he no longer touched her.

'And you, at least, have some colour in your cheeks now, my girl,' he grinned. 'Let's see if we can make it to the hospital before it fades.'

Which astonished Kate so much she was still fumbling to get her door shut when he started up the Range Rover and spun away from the layby, chuckling happily as if he was totally unaware of her anger and dismay.

It wasn't until they reached the hospital parking lot, only a few minutes later, that he spoke again.

'Forgetting this business of promises,' he said with a deliberate grin, 'I suggest we'd better at least agree on some sort of truce. Won't do Daddy any good to think we hate each other, will it?'

'He'll never guess,' Kate snarled. 'But if you ever again

lay a hand on me, I promise you'll regret it!'

'And I really believe you mean that, dear Kate,' Ben replied. 'So don't get all stroppy when I assist you from this vehicle—like any gentleman should. Just grin and bear it. Keeping up appearances, remember?'

'You wouldn't know a gentleman if you met one in your soup,' Kate replied with a broad grin that did nothing to mask the acid in her voice.

She was still wearing that grin an hour later when she, her father, and Benton Croft pulled up at the Kondalilla Falls restaurant for lunch. Kate would rather have gone straight back to the property, but she couldn't disrupt her father's obvious pleasure.

Mindful of Ben's warning, she had been able to stifle a cry of alarm at her father's haggard appearance when they had rushed into each other's arms at the hospital. Henry Lyle had aged greatly in the almost two years since Kate had last seen him, and although tanned from his outdoor work, he seemed thinner and somehow smaller than she remembered.

Or perhaps it was merely the comparison with the bulk of Ben Croft, who loomed over both of them with a sort of elderly benevolence that ignored the age difference between him and Henry.

It was almost as if Ben were the eldest, Kate decided, from the way her father deferred to him. And yet they were obviously the very best of friends, greeting each other with ribald familiarity and genuine affection.

'Well, I see Kate's made a big impression on you already, Ben,' her father jibed. 'Just look at you—even a tie, for goodness' sake! I'm sure you didn't get this prettied up just to impress me.'

'Oh, she's made an impression all right,' Ben replied with a broad smile for her father and a malicious, devilish little grin for Kate, who stared back at him angrily.

'Well, I can understand why,' said Henry Lyle. 'Although I must say, child, that you could do with a bit of fattening up. You look as if you've been off your feed for too long.'

'If you'd quit yapping and get in the truck, we might remedy that,' Ben interrupted, flinging open the door. 'It's to be Kondalilla Falls for lunch, and after two days of my own cooking, I'm ready for it!'

With Kate jammed between them, the two men bantered pleasantly all the way to the restaurant, usually in terms that focussed unwarranted attention on Kate. And, she quickly realised, on her present and future relationship with Benton Croft.

The lack of subtlety made it somewhat embarrassing, but her most immediate concern was her physical reaction to the man's proximity. His strong thigh kept brushing against her as he drove quickly on the twisting highway, and she began to wonder if he wasn't deliberately taking corners too quickly just so as to throw her against him.

They dined luxuriously on pâté Grand Marnier, frogs' legs and pork fillet and prawns in a spicy sauce, eating in relative silence as they all admired the spectacular view from the restaurant's picture windows, which looked away and down to the west from the ridgetop setting. Kate would have enjoyed the meal more without Ben's deliberate, taunting glances, but she was nonetheless impressed by the diversity of menu and the excellent food.

A walk down to look at the falls would have been pleasant, but Henry Lyle vetoed the idea with a suggestion that Kate might enjoy it more without a tired old man playing gooseberry. That hint was too broad to accept blandly, and she countered with the suggestion that she would return on her own one day.

'Nonsense!' Ben interjected surprisingly. 'Once we get you a bit more settled I'll take a day and show you all the sights.'

'Oh, no, I wouldn't think of taking you from your work,' Kate replied sweetly, hoping her father wouldn't notice the scathing look that accompanied the reply. Damn Ben Croft, anyway! It was bad enough that her father seemed determined to throw them at each other, without Ben blithely going along with him.

When they finally returned to Kathryn Downs, Kate's father declared an immediate need for a nap, suggesting that Ben spend the remainder of the afternoon showing Kate around the property.

Her efforts to refuse were blithely ignored and she was sent off to her room to change, carrying with her the memory of Ben's deliberate wink. She returned to find him back in worn blue jeans and a khaki shirt, and received a vague nod of approval at her own rough clothing and comfortable walking boots.

Her father had already disappeared to his room, but Ben greeted her effusively, as if Henry Lyle were still in the room, and gallantly held the door for her as they left the house.

His manner changed, however, once they had walked beyond hearing range of the big house, and the gallantry became a sort of mocking assertion of his control.

No matter that Kate started it; she expected the change and indeed forced it by immediately starting to rail at him.

'You are the most despicable, rotten, miserable swine I've ever met in my life!' she charged immediately they had gained the freedom of the loading yards. 'You're . . . deliberately playing up my father's ridiculous matchmaking—and don't you dare try to deny it!'

She was flushed with anger, her bosom heaving as she stood glaring up into those hateful green eyes, eyes that only laughed at her frustration while they deliberately undressed her.

'Why should I deny it?' he replied, and then, insolently, 'I've had worse offers, I suppose.'

'Well, just you get this straight,' Kate panted. 'There's no offer and there damned well won't ever be. I meant every word that I said earlier, and if you touch me again you'll be sorry!'

'And if you don't calm down I'll take you over my knee and paddle your little butt for you,' he growled. 'Just because everything isn't going your way there's no excuse for behaving like a spoilt child. I prefer my women to have a little class—and show it.'

'Well, I suppose one of you ought to,' she sneered. 'But since I'm not one of your women and don't intend to be, I'll talk as I damned well please, and if you don't like it you can lump it!'

And then she squealed in terror as he grabbed her up by the shoulders and shook her severely.

'Let's understand each other (shake!),' he growled. 'You (shake!) may say you're not my woman, (shake!) but your father obviously has (shake!) other ideas, which leaves me (shake!) with the casting vote. And I (shake!) reckon it might do you the world of good.

'Besides, if it makes your father happy I'm all in favour. He doesn't need the hassles of you and me at loggerheads. And therefore, dear Kate, you'll just have to accept the façade of my interest.'

A final shake almost made her teeth rattle, and when he finally set her down she was pasty-faced and trembling, barely able to focus on his final words.

'But don't worry about my taking unfair advantage; I

doubt if you'd be my type at the best of times—which these most definitely are not! Now settle down and get yourself under control. Just think of it all as a game; I do.'

And before she could reply he had taken her lightly by the arm and led her off on a walking tour of the property, describing the various features to her as if the earlier incident had never happened.

Kate stumbled along with him, still shaken by the ferocity she had seen in his eyes and now thoroughly confused by his abrupt change to informative, genial host.

She barely heard his comments about the loading yards and equipment, but when they reached the first deer paddock her own fascination triumphed over chagrin.

A small herd of red deer hinds, virtually all of them accompanied by smaller, brightly-spotted versions of themselves, trotted alertly around the paddock as Kate and Ben approached.

'Oh, how absolutely gorgeous!' she cried, eyes bright with pleasure at the pastoral sight. The spindly-legged, spotted calves and their ever-alert mothers looked up in fresh alarm at the sound of her voice, and some of them leapt quickly away from that side of the paddock.

'Oh . . . oh, my. I suppose I shouldn't have cried out?' Kate asked her tall companion, their earlier argument quite forgotten for the moment.

'Not to worry. This herd is fairly well used to people,' he replied with a slow grin. 'They're all farm-bred—not nearly so spooky as wild-caught deer.'

Even as he spoke, he kept them moving slowly along the race between two ranks of small paddocks, with those on the left side empty. The next paddock on the right, however, contained yet another surprise for Kate.

This paddock fairly seethed with majestic, beautiful fallow deer bucks, each with a spreading crown of many-pointed antlers. These animals were less excitable, apparently, than the hinds with their calves, and several moved up to the fence at Ben's approach, their fine muzzles twitching as if in welcome.

He spoke lightly to the boldest of the bucks, poking his fingers through the high, chain-mesh fencing so the deer could sniff at him.

'Hello, you rotten, treacherous old devil,' Ben whispered, seemingly unaware that Kate was close behind him and well within hearing. 'Oh, yes . . . you're a great sook now, aren't you? But in another couple of months you'll be trying to put me in hospital again. Well, you'll have to be lucky, old son, and if you get another chance you'd better make it good, or I'll turn you into hamburger without a second thought!'

The pretty, reddish animal with light spots across his rump and withers wrinkled up his lip as if laughing at Ben, then trotted haughtily away as the big man removed his fingers.

'What was all that about?' Kate asked curiously as they moved towards the next pen, which held a number of red deer stags browsing quietly, but without the enormous racks of antler she'd rather expected.

'Nothing serious,' was the reply. 'He tried to spike me to the fence during last season's rut, but this year I'll be ready for him.'

'But he looks so . . . so gentle,' Kate replied, not really in protest, but rather bewildered. The tiny little fallow buck had been only about three feet high, and with his fragile legs and beatific expression appeared to be no great threat to a man of Ben's stature.

'Don't you believe it,' Ben replied, and then turned to face her, his eyes bleak with stark sincerity. 'Don't *ever* even think it,' he cautioned. '*All* deer can be dangerous, even the does and hinds. And during the rut, some stags would take great delight in killing you. Remember that!'

'You are serious, aren't you?' Kate mused. 'You're not just having me on?'

Ben's laugh was harsh, and far from reassuring. 'Remind me to show you the scars some time,' he replied. 'Yes, dear Kate, I'm deadly serious. They've got hooves like razors and no compunction about using them, especially if they're cornered or angry. Now I know you hate to promise me anything, but this is no joke. You're not ever, under any circumstances, to go into any paddock, not without somebody along who knows what's going on. Is that clear?'

His expression defied argument. 'Yes,' Kate said. 'Yes, I understand.'

'I bloody well hope so,' he replied. 'You're much too pretty to take chances like that.'

And he walked on without seeming to notice the surprise Kate registered at the quite unexpected compliment. Surprise . . . and pleasure, though she didn't like to admit that, even to herself and certainly never ever to Ben Croft.

As they continued their tour, he explained the general operation of the farm, including why the red deer stags, all but one enormous creature, had no antlers.

'Deer farming is still in its infancy in Australia,' he explained, 'and only slightly more mature in New Zealand, where it started really moving during the 70s. But the future potential is truly staggering, when you consider that virtually every aspect of the beast is marketable. Including some parts,' he added with a wry grin, 'that you'd never expect.'

'I *have* heard of the rather unorthodox uses for deer antlers in the Orient,' Kate replied somewhat frostily, not wishing to be thought totally ignorant despite the fact that she very nearly was.

'Oh, have you?' Ben replied with a mischievous light in his eyes. 'As an aphrodisiac, no doubt.' And he chuckled wickedly. 'Maybe we'll have to let you try some, one day, or don't you believe it would work?'

'I haven't the faintest idea, nor do I particularly want to find out,' she replied coldly, wishing she could pull her eyes away from his distinctly masculine stare. It was both frustrating and frightening the way he could so vividly affect her without so much as actual physical contact.

'Just as well,' he replied laughingly, 'because the idea of antlers as an aphrodisiac is nothing but a load of Western rubbish. Rhinoceros horn? Well, who really knows? But not antlers. In fact they're processed purely for their medicinal value.'

Kate's face must have revealed her distaste, but Ben merely laughed even louder.

'Actually, however, I think the real future is in the velvet, which is also used for medicines. All these deer you've seen today, especially the stags, are worth a helluva lot more alive than in any meat market. A big red deer stag can produce four to five kilograms of velvet, and keep on doing it year after year. In Poland there are monsters who produce as much as thirteen kilograms, but I've never seen one of those.

'Right at the moment, the velvet market's not the best because the Russians seem to have undercut it badly, but that won't go on for ever and there's still a fair profit to be made. Especially since deer farming is still a growth industry, and there's a ready market for seed stock right round Australia.

'If you'd arrived a few months earlier, you'd have seen how we handle the velvet, but I've got some frozen stuff you can have a look at if you're interested.'

'Just so long as I don't have to eat it,' Kate replied,

turning up her lip. She had the unholy feeling he was merely toying with her, and made a mental note to ask her father about all Ben had told her.

'Not a chance,' he said, 'although when it's been dried it gets sliced up into something very similar to potato crisps that are almost worth their weight in gold on the retail market.'

'Thanks just the same,' she said with a negative shake of her head.

'Well, at least after last night I know you like venison, so you're not a total loss,' he retorted. 'Just don't develop too much of a taste for it, because our deer are too valuable alive for us to be eating them. And speaking of food, you'd best head back to the house now and think about digging out something for tea. I forgot to get anything from the freezer this morning, so you'll probably have to cook in the microwave, which I presume you know how to use.'

'I've never used one in my life, but I imagine I'll be able to manage all right,' she replied staunchly. 'Judging from the size of the lunch you ate, I don't suppose you'll want dinner until fairly late anyway.'

'Not too late. I need my beauty sleep,' he replied with a grin. 'And so do you. You're starting to look awfully pale again.'

Kate backed away hastily, but he made no attempt to kiss the colour back into her cheeks again. Instead, frustratingly, he stepped back himself and laughed at her fright.

'Good reflexes you've got,' he chuckled. 'Too bad you forgot I've been warned off on threat of dire punishment.'

'Too bad you're not enough of a gentleman so the warning wouldn't be necessary,' she snapped, somewhat unsure whether she was angry because he hadn't tried to kiss her, or because he had so accutately read her intentions.

'I'm gentleman enough when I want to be,' he replied, 'but I think you'd get bored with a man who was too gentle too often.'

'I'd rather be bored than constantly in fear of being mauled,' Kate replied soberly. 'It's not something I very much enjoy.'

'So I noticed,' he replied dryly. 'What did your husband do—set you up on a pedestal and beg permission before he kissed you?'

'That is absolutely none of your business,' Kate replied, suddenly wary.

His grin was devilish. 'Why not? If your father's going to be so determined to match us up, I'm surely entitled to know what I'm up against.'

'What you're up against is nothing at all,' Kate snapped, her patience suddenly gone. 'I don't care what my father is trying to accomplish. I won't be thrown at you or any other man.'

'Especially me,' he agreed. 'What are you going to do, spend the remainder of your life in love with a memory?'

In *love* with a memory? Kate shivered, shaken by the possibility. If she had ever had love for Wayne, he had killed it long before dying himself, but he had also killed—or very nearly so—her image of herself as a woman. And better that too should be dead, she thought, than for it to be so rudely reawakened by this antagonistic, autocratic stranger.

She would have her memories, all right. But love, the kind of love she had often dreamed of, the kind she could react to, was neither in her memories nor in the liaison her father seemed to imagine for her with Ben Croft.

'No, Mr Croft, I'm not in love with a memory,' she replied then, with a candour that surprised her—and stopped. She hadn't meant to say that. She'd meant to say something entirely different, something which would keep Ben Croft at arm's length or further. Because he was dangerous. Dangerous to her peace of mind, to the fragility of her own self-image.

In love with a memory! She *hated* her memories, and most especially the memory of wishing her husband dead and having her wish fulfilled. Even Wayne, swine that he was, didn't deserve that. And yet? Alive he had done his best to destroy her, and now that he was dead he somehow was coming even closer to success.

'Damn it! You're doing that again.' Ben's harsh voice grated across her consciousness, pulling her back to the present, to open her eyes and see blazing green orbs devouring her.

He reached out and took her by the shoulders, and for an instant Kate feared he was going to shake her again. But instead his eyes lost their hellish glow and his voice, when he spoke, was soft with compassion.

'Where do you go, I wonder?' he said. 'And why, since it obviously hurts you so?'

The touch of his fingers was feather-light, and for an aeon Kate stood there, half inclined to fling herself into his arms and cry. But she couldn't, and finally she flung herself instead into freedom, stumbling away from him and shaking her head wildly.

'Damn you! I told you never to touch me again,' she cried, and then continued to shriek at him, hearing his voice as he spoke to her, but not allowing the words to penetrate.

She turned and fled back along the wide race between the deer paddocks, and it wasn't until she reached the relative sanctity of the handling yards, where the solid walls and roof shut out the mid-afternoon sunlight and provided a cool, almost peaceful atmosphere, that she halted and leaned panting against the boards.

Ben Croft hadn't followed her. He stood, tall and immobile in the harshness of the sun, looking after her. Unsmiling, his strong face a mask of planes and shadows beneath the broad brim of his hat, he stood like a statue until Kate had finally regained sufficient composure to turn away and walk through the yards towards the house. Thinking about it later, she wondered at his reaction, because her mind had recalled his final words, and they had been words not of anger, but of genuine sorrow at her fright.

And they were far kinder words than many used by her father when he came and sat talking to her in the kitchen while she prepared dinner that evening.

If the dinner was an unqualified culinary success, Kate's first conversation with her father alone was anything but.

CHAPTER THREE

'WHY don't you like Ben Croft?'

Her father's first words as he sat himself easily—and backwards—on a kitchen chair, leaning his arms on the high back and soberly observing Kate for her reaction, did nothing to ease the confusion she was feeling within herself.

'I don't dislike him,' Kate replied, hedging deliberately. It was a wasted gesture; Henry Lyle knew his daughter too well.

'Are you just off men entirely because of Wayne, or is it something personal between you and Ben?'

'My God!' she cried. 'What is this—the Spanish Inquisition? I don't get a *hello*, or a *how are you*, or *Gee, it's good to see you*. Just a bunch of silly questions about a man I only met less than twenty-four hours ago. Really, Daddy, how could you expect me to know if I like him or not in that short a time?'

'I seem to remember you had yourself thoroughly infatuated with Wayne within twenty-four hours of meeting him,' her father replied acidly. Definitely, thought Kate, a very low blow. 'And you and Ben didn't fool me one little bit during lunch and the drive home. Let me assure you of that, young lady. Now I want to know what's going on, and I want to know now!'

'There is nothing going on,' Kate snapped. 'And nobody was trying to fool you about anything.' Only, she thought, a small lie. 'If you saw anything, it was embarrassment from both of us at your idiotic attempts to thrust us together.'

A larger lie, that one. But at least partially effective. Provided, of course, that her father didn't suddenly remember that Ben Croft hadn't been remotely embarrassed by the blatant matchmaking. Amused, certainly, but hardly embarrassed.

'Well, why shouldn't I try to throw you together? Ben's ten thousand times the man Wayne was. He'd be a damned good match for you.'

'I don't suppose it's occurred to anybody—including you—that I'm more than capable of choosing my own man, assuming I might want one in the first place?'

'Not on past experience,' he replied sarcastically. 'Or did your so-called marriage at least teach you a little better taste?'

Kate's jaw dropped. Gone was any thought of deceiving her father; he obviously knew far more about her intimate secrets than she could have imagined. Or, she thought suddenly, did he?

'Just exactly what are you getting at?' she queried, cocking her head to one side and fixing her parent with a stern glance.

'Well, you weren't happy with Wayne, were you?' he countered, and Kate's heart sang. He *didn't* know! He was bluffing, up to his old tricks. And she'd nearly fallen for it.

'I really don't know how you can say that,' she replied, equally evasively. 'Nor do I quite understand why you insist on speaking ill of the dead.'

'Nothing I wouldn't have said when he was alive—and to his face, if he'd ever had the guts to face me,' her father snorted. 'Not that he ever would, being nothing but a ratbag and a scoundrel. But of course you already know that, don't you, Kate?'

'Frankly, I don't see that it's important anyway, since he's dead,' she replied. 'Much less do I see what it has to do with Ben Croft. Or,' she added with serious emphasis, 'with any other man. If you've got some pipedream about marrying me off to the first man that comes along, you can just forget it, because I'm not interested. Is that clear?'

'Abundantly,' her father replied, suddenly, suspiciously calm again. Kate shied at that, knowing only too well that Henry Lyle angry and argumentative was far less dangerous than the same father in a calm, speculative mood.

'Besides,' she added rather lamely, 'I've only been widowed for three months. Don't you think it's a little bit early to be shopping again?'

'Bulldust!' her father snapped. 'It's the people who've been most happily married that adjust the best when their partner dies. I was shopping again damned quick after your mother died, just as she *expected* me to. It was her fondest wish that I remarry and be as happy as I was with her; she told me so herself on her very deathbed.'

Kate's surprise was in no way feigned. She hadn't been aware of her father so much as looking at another woman during the three years since her mother's death. She didn't know what to say.

'Oh, I suppose you're going to ask why I haven't re-married myself during the last three years,' Henry Lyle continued, apparently oblivious to his daughter's astonishment. 'It's because I haven't met anybody who's half the woman your mother was, and that's it in a nutshell. But I've been lonely, Kate, so lonely you wouldn't imagine it, sometimes. And I don't want that for you, not on top of . . .' His voice trailed off, then returned more strongly.

'And damn it, I'm sorry for jumping on you like this, and maybe even for thrusting you and Ben together. It's just that—my God, you look so harassed and run down. You don't take good enough care of yourself.'

His own weariness had suddenly surged forth into control again, and Kate flung her arms around him with a cry of exasperation.

'At least nobody has to send me into hospital for a rest,' she chided gently. 'And now I'm here, so neither of us will be lonely and we'll both get plenty of rest.'

Then both of them were silent for a time, each simply content with being together again as father and daughter. Only when her cooking chores demanded it did Kate finally shift back to her work, shooing her father off to sit on the porch with his pipe.

'But just you remember—no more of this matchmaking or I'll start doing some of my own,' she scolded as he left the room.

She had no sooner turned around when a too-familiar voice quipped, 'That's a helluva fine idea. I wish I'd thought of it.'

Ben Croft stood just outside the back door, mocking Kate with those horrible green eyes as he lifted off his hat and nodded agreeably. 'Mind if I come in?'

'Certainly not,' she retorted, trying to stifle her anger. How much had he heard? How long had he been standing there, spying on them?

'If it's any consolation, I only heard your parting remark,' he said without being asked. 'Although I can probably reconstruct the rest of the conversation from that, if you'd like.'

'Don't bother!' she snapped. And shooting him her most venomous glare, she turned her back deliberately and returned to her work.

He didn't reply, nor did he touch her as he squeezed past on his way to join her father, though Kate felt a slight tug near her waist. It wasn't until she turned to pick something up from the table and her apron fell down that she realised what he had done.

Her oath was more in amusement than anger, piqued by the memory of her mother's similar comments every time her father had surreptitiously untied apron strings with the same result.

I think maybe you're *too* well house-trained, Ben Croft, Kate thought, and spent the rest of her time in the kitchen wondering what woman in his life had got close enough to prompt that little trick. His mother, or . . . Kate was mildly surprised to find herself seriously wondering at the alternatives.

There was further evidence of Ben's house training when Kate called the men in to dinner some time later. In the interim he had obviously showered and—surprisingly—shaved, and he arrived at table dressed casually but with a certain elegance.

And during the meal he kept them both thoroughly and

often hilariously entertained with tales of his wanderings throughout south-east Asia, first during his military service and then as a self-styled entrepreneur. For the first time, Kate found herself able to really relax in his company, and she couldn't help noticing his gracious manners and ease of conversation. Without the tensions between them, his eyes were surrounded by laughter wrinkles and his undeniably handsome though rugged face softened almost to boyishness when he laughed himself.

Henry Lyle, fortunately, had abandoned his matchmaking, and Ben, it seemed, had decided to give up his habit of looking at Kate as if she were some kind of edible delicacy. Relaxation in both their company was easy.

Too easy! Almost without realising it, Kate found herself drifting into that dreamy lassitude which often presages sleep. And though some senses were dulled, others seemed more alive, more vibrant.

Her eyes lost their focus and her mind drifted from the conversation around her into a soft-textured world of its own. Yet her sense of smell was heightened, clearly picking up Ben's after-shave from across the room, the smell of fresh-perked coffee, of the flowers outside the window.

Kate didn't need to consciously watch Ben to nonetheless *see* him. In her mind she could pick out his features all too easily, not only as he appeared this night, but as he had appeared to her on the rain-drenched night of her arrival and even when he had so savagely kissed her during the trip to town. Especially, she realised, when he had kissed her.

Her eyes flew open with the realisation, and she was somewhat surprised to find that she had caught Ben surveying her from his position across the room.

He didn't look away guiltily, as she might have known, but instead his expression altered from one of almost benign fondness to his more normal sexual assessment. It was Kate's eyes that dropped away first.

Then her father began speaking again, and Kate looked to find Ben had switched his attentions, leaving her to her own thoughts.

And what thoughts they were! What, she wondered, had been responsible for his velvet-soft glance, the one she had caught him in by suddenly opening her eyes? Certainly it had no foundation in his treatment of her, where he had varied from accepting her as either spoiled child or frigid, selfish woman.

It continued to niggle at her when, a few moments later, both men decided bedtime had arrived, and everyone said their goodnights and wandered off to respective bedrooms. Kate was still considering that look, despite being half asleep, when she heard the telephone ring and leapt from her bed to run out into the hall and down the stairway to answer it.

She only got halfway down the stairs, however, before the ringing stopped and she heard Ben's unmistakable voice in reply.

Kate had no intention of eavesdropping, but almost from the first his words commanded her attention. From that moment, retreat became unthinkable.

'You'll come, then?' said Ben with obvious satisfaction, 'Fantastic, mate! The way things are developing around here, we can definitely use a manager like you.'

Then his voice seemed to slide off in the distance as Kate's horror rang in her ears. Manager? But her father, she thought, was the manager of Kathryn Downs. Or was he? She didn't know the exact financial arrangements of the partnership, but could it be possible Ben Croft was about to slough off his partner—his partner of questionable health—in favour of somebody else?

'. . . two weeks? Great! We'll look forward to seeing both of you,' Ben said. 'See you then, and give Robyn my love.'

And as she heard the telephone receiver being replaced, Kate fled to her room only in time to avoid meeting Ben Croft in the upstairs hallway. She returned to her bed, but sleep was impossible now; her mind was totally occupied with worry for both her father and herself.

She finally did sleep, after an age wondering about the significance of the telephone call. Who had Ben been talking to? And who was this Robyn, to whom he sent his love? But in the morning, waking from her restless slumber earlier than she had anticipated, Kate was no closer to knowing.

She dressed hurriedly and arrived in the kitchen before either of the men, and had the coffee ready and breakfast laid out just as Ben stepped into the room, dressed as usual in khaki work gear.

'Morning,' he smiled. And Kate murmured her own greeting with no such evidence of happiness. But her suspicion must have shown itself as something else, because Ben merely shot her a curious glance, then sat down to his coffee and remained silent for some time before speaking up.

'You look as if you didn't sleep well.'

'Well enough,' she replied somewhat curtly. 'Except that the phone woke me just as I was dropping off, and I had a bit of trouble getting back to sleep again.'

'Ah,' he responded. And then, damnably, shut up again.

'Was it . . . important?' Kate finally asked haltingly. She shivered inside at her temerity, but she just *had* to know more about that phone call. Everything, it seemed, might depend on it.

'Damned important . . . and damned good news as well,'
Ben replied, and once again relapsed into silence. Clearly
he wasn't about to enlighten her, and Kate felt herself
growing tense with concealed anger.

Damn the man! she thought, flinging herself about the
kitchen as she attempted to use up physical energy to
combat the heightening tensions within.

Once or twice she caught Ben glancing at her curiously,
but he made no further attempt at conversation, which
only made Kate even more angry.

Obviously, she thought, his disloyalty to her father
should reveal some evidence of guilt, and yet Ben sat at his
breakfast like the epitome of innocence, eating heartily
and with evident gusto.

It wasn't until Henry Lyle finally appeared, with a
vague apology for his lateness, that Ben bothered to indulge
in conversation.

'Bill and Robyn Campbell should be here within a fort-
night,' he said, quite unexpectedly to Kate's astonished
ears.

'Excellent,' her father replied, and her surprise increased. 'Things have developed to the point where we
can certainly use a man of his expertise.'

Almost exactly Ben's words of the night before! And,
obviously, the result of that late-night phone call was no
real surprise to Henry Lyle. Kate's confusion was unnerv-
ing, and it must have shown on her face as she poured
coffee for her father and a refill for Ben.

'I gather Ben hasn't explained,' Henry said. 'Not that
there's much to it. We're bringing in a friend of Ben's from
New Zealand as manager here. Ben thinks I don't know
that it's partly to take the work load off my shoulders . . .'

'Ben thinks you damned well should know that it's
almost entirely to take the work load off your shoulders,'

the tall, younger man retorted in mock anger. 'You didn't
come into this partnership to work yourself to death.' He
glanced at Kate, then shot her a surprising wink before
continuing. 'Besides, at your age it's brains that count, not
muscle.'

'At my age?' Henry Lyle snorted angrily. 'Damn it,
Ben, I'm only ... what? ... five years older than this
Campbell ...'

'Six,' Ben replied calmly. 'But let's not forget that you
spent twenty years as an advertising executive—Bill's
grown up doing hard physical labour. Hell, he could even
outwork *me* without breathing hard!'

Kate, growing more and more confused by the entire
dialogue, finally butted in with a comment of her own.
'Well, I'd certainly like to know more about this,' she
blurted. 'I thought *Dad* was the manager here.'

'And you're worried that I'm trying to ease him out,' Ben
retorted blithely. 'My God, but you're a suspicious woman;
it'll be great having Robyn here just for the contrast.'

Whereupon he rose from his seat and stalked towards
the doorway. 'You explain it to her, Henry,' he said. 'I'm
afraid I just can't be bothered.'

He was gone before Henry Lyle turned to his daughter
with a look of obvious intolerance on his face.

'Well done, Kate,' he growled. 'What is it with you and
Ben that you have to go out of your way to offend him?'

'Offend him? What is it with you that you can sit there
so calmly and let him shove you aside in favour of somebody else? Somebody you obviously don't even know,' she
continued. 'I heard him last night on the ... the telephone.
I wasn't really eavesdropping, either,' she added hastily,
'And he sounded just so delighted to be getting this ... this
Campbell person in here ...'

'As he damned well should be. I certainly am,' her

father interrupted. 'For God's sake stop being so defensive of your poor old dad! I'm not exactly an invalid, and frankly I resent it. Just so you'll know—Campbell's coming has been part of the plan right from the beginning. He's one of the most astute New Zealand deer farming experts there is, although he's never had the money to get in on his own bat. Ben and I have always intended to bring him in as a one-third partner, but not until we'd expanded to the point where he could honestly contribute enough of his expertise and labour to pay his own way. He's a proud man, from what I'm told, and I think it was damned diplomatic of Ben to organise things as he's done.'

He paused, seemingly to let Kate get a word in edgewise, but resumed speaking before she could open her mouth.

'And as for you, young lady, I think you'd best reorganise your thinking about Ben Croft and the entire situation here. Ben is one of nature's gentlemen, and I'm not amused at the way you two keep striking sparks off each other. Do I make myself perfectly clear?'

'You do indeed,' she replied humbly. 'And now I realise how you got so high in the advertising world. I've never had such a ticking off in my life. Not that I didn't deserve it,' she hastened, 'and I shall apologise to B ... Mr Croft for everything, honestly I will. It's just that ... that I got the feeling I was supposed to be looking after you ... and ...'

'And you got a little carried away. And I understand, and I'm sorry I rousted on you,' her father replied tenderly. 'It's just that I ... I sort of hoped you and Ben would hit it off properly. In fact it's probably my fault that you didn't, as you said earlier.'

'No, it wasn't exactly that,' Kate replied. 'I just don't think we were meant to ... hit it off properly, as you say. But not to worry, I'll get things straightened out, and even cook you both something special for dinner as an added apology.'

Which she did, later that day, although the dinner apology was somewhat more successful than the personal one she afforded Ben after spending half an hour seeking him out that morning.

'Forget it,' was his brusque reply. And to Kate's now-guilty conscience there was no friendliness in those dark, brooding green eyes.

'But . . .' She might as well not have spoken.

'I said forget it. Now if you'll excuse me?' And he was gone, striding away from her without a backward glance.

'Damn the man,' she thought later as she mixed the ingredients of a cake in the quiet kitchen. 'Damn!'

By dinner time it seemed Ben's anger had cooled; he was at least moderately polite, if not the congenial personage of the evening before.

But he was no nearer to accepting Kate's second attempt at an apology.

'I said to forget it, and that's what I meant,' he growled. 'As far as I'm concerned the subject is closed.'

'Well, all right,' Kate replied. 'But I . . .'

'Closed! Over . . . finished . . . done,' he interrupted. 'And if you don't shut up about it, I won't take you out to meet our fence patrols tomorrow.'

'What fence patrols?' Kate asked, but the question drew only a knowing chuckle from the two men, who both refused to enlighten her.

'You're setting me up for something,' she accused, but even that drew no satisfactory response.

'The other thing Kate might do is help you evaluate what's to be done at the other house,' said Henry Lyle, turning the conversation neatly away from Kate's questions. 'Now that Campbell's sister has decided to come along, I'm sure they'd prefer living on their own.'

'If Kate doesn't mind, I'd welcome her advice,' Ben replied. And this time, Kate's questions got reasonable answers.

The 'other house' was an overseer's cottage tucked away behind a small grove of trees which created privacy despite the cottage's proximity to the main house.

'It hasn't been lived in for several years, but it'll be a nice little place once it's cleaned up,' Ben mused. 'I'll see if we can hire somebody from town to come out and do that, once we've established what's needed.'

'Surely I can do it,' Kate suggested. 'Please . . . I've very little else to do.'

'Apart from feeding us and keeping this monstrosity in order, you mean,' Ben replied. 'And don't go telling me there's nothing to it; it's obvious you've been cooking and cleaning in here all day long, with splendid results.'

'Thank you,' she smiled, inordinately pleased at the compliment. 'But really there *isn't* much to it. Both you and Dad are reasonably tidy people, and besides, you're hardly ever here. It's not as if the house was filled with children or anything.'

'No,' Ben agreed, 'although that's what this bloody great barn of a place really needs—about half a dozen kids running around everywhere. Maybe we'll have to organise your dad a wife, and set them to work filling the place.'

Both he and Kate laughed at Henry Lyle sputtering out his opposition to the suggestion, but their laughter died quickly when he suggested that either or both of them would be more logical candidates.

'I've had my child-raising days,' he said, 'and you can see what a mess of it I made.'

Kate bristled at the criticism, but it was Ben who spoke out against it.

'I think you've done rather well, myself,' he grinned. 'A little sparing of the rod, perhaps, but give her the right man and a couple of kids and she'd be a winner.'

'Well, thank you very much—I think,' Kate retorted. 'Now if you two are all through planning my life for me, perhaps you'd like to adjourn to the lounge so I can clear away in here.'

Her father took the suggestion eagerly, but Ben lagged behind as the older man left the room. 'I'll hang about and help you wash up,' he said.

'You'll do no such thing,' Kate replied, only to be blithely ignored as he filled the sink and began scrubbing.

'You can dry,' he said, once again ignoring her objections. 'And if it worries you, I don't plan on making a habit of this, but tonight I feel like washing dishes.'

The rest of the task was completed in silence. Ben concentrated on his scrubbing and Kate, with nothing to say, stood at his side and dried everything as it came from the sink.

Because of his help, the task took only a few minutes, but it was later, when she was tucked away in her bed, that Kate's mind dwelt on the unexpected pleasure she had really felt at sharing work of that type with a man. It was obvious Ben Croft was no stranger to kitchen chores, and she wondered idly if he cared entirely for himself when at home, wherever that was, or if he had a housekeeper. Or . . . somebody who was rather more than a housekeeper?

That thought brought an unexpected twinge of annoyance, and she quickly thrust it aside. None of her business anyway, she mused, and fell asleep wondering about it just the same.

She slept fitfully, mostly because of incessant subcon-

scious reminders that she must be up and ready to go early
if she was to accompany Ben on his pre-dawn patrol of the
fence-lines with their mysterious guardians.

The sun was still asleep when Kate stumbled through
the still-dark hallway to the kitchen, but Ben Croft was
there ahead of her, with the coffee already made.

'Even hot water for tea, if you'd rather,' he said softly
after bidding her good morning.

'Coffee's fine, and thank you for getting it,' Kate replied.
'I'm sorry I got up too late . . .'

'None of that,' he interrupted with a grin. 'I got up
earlier than usual; you weren't late at all.'

'How early is usual?' Kate asked, not really caring
except for the need of idle conversation to break the dawn
stillness.

'Sun-up, out here,' he replied. 'A bit later when I'm at
home, because I'm usually up a fair bit later at night.
Personally, I prefer it out here, but custom seems to have
dictated that the business of the world is done in cities, so
I've little real choice.'

Kate smiled. 'I'm glad things worked out so that I could
get away from the city. This place is heaven after Melbourne—I'm already in love with it.'

'Even this enormous house?' He asked the question quite
seriously.

'Oh, yes!' she replied eagerly. 'It's a lovely old house,
just perfect for the setting. Although,' she mused, 'I rather
have to agree with your comments last night. It's certainly
a bit large for just the three of us.'

'Well, maybe you'll miss me when I'm gone, after all,'
he replied with a wicked grin.

'I quite likely shall,' Kate replied sweetly, refusing to be
drawn. 'When are you leaving?'

'Probably tomorrow,' he replied, and grinned even

wider at her involuntary exclamation of surprise. 'I do have other business interests,' he said. 'This place is actually the least of them—sort of a planned retirement programme, if you like.'

'I wouldn't have thought you were quite old enough for retirement,' Kate replied, glancing slyly over the top of her coffee cup.

'I'm thirty-six, so you can stop fishing,' he replied. 'And I believe retirement should be taken while you're young enough to enjoy it, not when you're too old to do anything else. So I take mine in bits and pieces as I go along.'

'Nice work if you can get it,' she quipped, 'but if you retire when you're young, what does it leave when you're older?'

Ben laughed. 'A rocking chair by a trout stream, with a sturdy young wife to fetch and carry for me and two dozen kids to run the farm, maybe,' he replied.

'Two dozen? You don't want a wife, you want a brood mare!' Kate exclaimed.

His first reply was a casually-raised eyebrow. 'Well . . . maybe not quite two dozen. But a couple, anyway. Being an only child must be horribly lonely.'

'Now who's fishing?' she chided. 'But you're right. I think two is a nice number.'

'You wouldn't go to seven, I suppose?'

'Seven! My God! Is that how many there were in your family? I don't envy your mother.'

Ben grinned ruefully. 'There were usually about thirty in my family, if you could call it that,' he replied. 'I was raised in an orphanage.'

'Oh,' said Kate. 'I'm . . . I'm sorry.'

'Don't be. It didn't do me any great harm, in the long run. Anyway, let's be away now. There's a lot of fence-line to walk before breakfast.'

They strolled together along the wide corridor between the paddock fences and the strong, high boundary fence, but Ben spoke no more of his childhood. Instead he explained about the specialised construction of the deer farm fences.

The boundary fence was more than six feet high, with foot netting of tarred mesh lying on the ground both inside and outside. That, he explained, was to keep deer from trying to slip out underneath, and keep digging animals like foxes or dogs from getting in.

'But the real protection is on the way now,' he said, waving to draw Kate's attention to the shadowy figures emerging from the mist of a hollow not far ahead.

She cried out in astonishment and delight. 'Donkeys! You don't mean it.'

'I certainly do,' he replied gravely. 'They're not only a profitable sideline, since there's a growing interest in donkey breeding these days, but they're damned good guardians for the deer. They'll run off any stray dogs as quick as you please, and quite often serve a Judas role when we have to shift deer from one paddock to another.'

'I don't understand.'

'Well, you can't drive deer like sheep or cattle. You can only sort of encourage them to wander along where you want them to go. If they're pushed too hard, they spook and try to get back where they've been. But we've found that once they get used to the idea, they'll tend to follow the donkeys from one paddock to another, and the donkeys, of course, are quite easy to induce with food.'

That much, at least, was evident. The approaching donkeys had switched to a trot as they recognised Ben, and soon the two humans were surrounded by gently probing muzzles as the donkeys began scrounging for the apples Ben had brought with him.

'Don't leave anything sticking out of your pockets,' he warned Kate. 'These little beggars will steal anything that isn't tied down. They got my wallet a few days ago, and it took an hour of chasing to get it back.'

The idea of six-foot-one Ben Croft chasing a mischievous, speedy little donkey brought peals of laughter from Kate, but it was Ben's turn to laugh a moment later when one of the younger beasts filched Kate's headscarf right off her head and trotted happily away with it.

'Don't say I didn't warn you,' he chuckled as she tried futilely to catch the culprit. 'And there's no sense chasing him; try and lure him back with a bit of apple.'

It took the two of them fifteen minutes of combined chasing and bribery to rescue the headscarf, and by the end of it they were both almost helpless with laughter that kept recurring during the rest of their escorted fence patrol.

By the time they returned to the house, Kate was still bubbling with happiness, and she turned at the doorway to thank Ben.

'It was the nicest morning I've spent in . . . I don't know how long,' she said, eyes shining and cheeks flushed with pleasure.

'I'm glad,' he said softly, and before she realised what was afoot he had reached out to tip up her chin and kiss her, ever so lightly, on the lips. 'And I enjoyed it too,' he said then, and stepped back to hold the door for her.

Kate hummed happily as she prepared breakfast for them all, and was still humming when the men had departed and she was alone with her housework. It *had* been a great morning, she decided, and that oh-so-gentle kiss wasn't exactly the least of reasons for it.

He didn't repeat the exercise that afternoon, when the two of them strolled over to inspect the manager's cottage.

But he was pleasant, charming, and—Kate decided later—very, very comfortable to be with.

They decided on what was needed without even a hint of argument, although Ben repeated his offer to hire the work done rather than place the load on Kate.

'Nonsense,' she retorted. 'It's only a matter of a few days spent cleaning, and of course painting that lounge room and kitchen.'

'It'll be a lot of work,' he said.

'Of course it will, but I didn't come here for a rest cure, did I?' she replied. 'And whatever my other faults, I'm not afraid of getting my hands dirty, you know?'

'Steady on, lady! Nobody's accusing you of anything,' he grinned. 'All I'm saying is that I appreciate your taking the time, and I'm sure Bill and Robyn will, too.'

Kate's pulse raced at the gentle appreciation in his glance, and she had to turn away quickly because of a distinct risk that she would burst into tears.

Why, she thought, should this tall man's approval have suddenly become so important to her? The fact that Wayne hadn't shown much approval of anything she did might certainly contribute, but even that couldn't account for the pleasure Ben Croft could give with a simple compliment . . . or a simple look.

Yet when Ben left for Brisbane the next morning, Kate soon found that she actually missed him. She took on the fence patrol herself each morning during his absence, and every mischievous moment spent with her donkey companions merely served to help her relive that first, glorious morning.

The rest of the time she was too busy to give much thought to her feelings. The manager's cottage proved to be even more of a task than she had originally thought, and she spent every spare moment in cleaning and fixing up the cottage. Having painted the kitchen and lounge, she decided the rest of the rooms looked dingy, so she made another trip to town for more supplies, and painted the entire cottage inside and out.

By the day of Ben's return, she was exhausted but highly pleased with herself. If this Campbell fellow was as important as Ben and her father thought, he would at least be assured of a warm welcome by the appearance of his new home.

Kate had no idea when they would be arriving, but she had found an enormous pork roast in the freezer, and spent the day putting together a mammoth welcoming dinner. She had just popped the roast in the oven, in fact, when the phone rang.

'Kate?' The deep, rich voice sent shivers down her spine, but the message wasn't nearly so pleasant. Ben would be held up in Brisbane, and Bill and Robyn Campbell would be arriving by themselves, probably just before dinner hour.

'I'm really sorry I can't make it, but I'm sure you can handle introductions without me,' he said. 'They're both friendly, genuine people and they're looking forward to meeting you.'

'Oh, I'm sure there won't be any problems,' Kate replied with an assurance she didn't quite feel. Or was it more accurately a feeling of disappointment that Ben wouldn't be there for her special dinner? 'Everything's ready at the cottage,' she concluded rather lamely, 'and I've got a huge roast cooking for when they arrive.'

'Good girl,' he said. 'I knew I could count on you. See you when I get there, then . . . probably in a couple of days. Bill is bringing up my Range Rover, so I may have to arrange for somebody to pick me up at the airport. I'll let you know, in any event.'

Kate hung up the phone with a dull ache building in her stomach, and immediately chided herself for the feelings. It was ridiculous, she decided, that having objected so strongly to her father's matchmaking attempts, she should now start reacting as if they'd worked.

Worse than ridiculous, because she neither wanted nor needed another man in her life, not even one as impressive as Ben Croft.

She tried during the rest of the afternoon to get it out of her mind, and was glad she had, when Bill Campbell and his sister Robyn arrived just at dusk.

Bill Campbell was roughly what Kate had expected, a tall, lean, rugged-looking man of about fifty with 'outdoors' written all over him.

His sister Robyn, however, was quite something else again.

CHAPTER FOUR

ROBYN CAMPBELL was, quite simply, beautiful. No other word could so completely describe the dark-haired, dark-eyed vision that stepped from the Range Rover and advanced upon Kate and her father with a bright smile.

Slightly shorter than Kate, and not nearly so slender, she had a voluptuous figure, a warm smile, and a gentle, genuine friendliness that couldn't be ignored.

On anyone else it might have been termed gushy, but Robyn's extrovert nature and outgoing personality allowed her to *ooh* and *aah* over her new home, the big house shared by Kate and her father, and Kate's admittedly excellent dinner without seeming in the least affected.

'You really shouldn't have gone to so much trouble,' she said once they were seated at dinner. 'It's made me feel most dreadfully spoiled ... first a week in Brisbane with Ben, and now this. It'll take me a week to settle down.'

It became quickly clear that Robyn was the outgoing one in the family. 'I do the talking for both of us,' she'd quipped with a grin at her taciturn but friendly older brother. Older, but by how much? Kate wondered. Her expectation of Robyn as some sort of spinster sister had been rudely jolted by this vision of mature loveliness, and she forced herself in fairness to put Robyn's age at no more than thirty-five.

A spinster, perhaps ... but hardly through anything but choice, Kate thought. And wondered about that week in Brisbane with Ben.

It was only too obvious that he and Robyn were, at the very least, good friends. Good friends ... and how much more? she wondered, and then mentally rebuked herself for such thoughts. Besides, it was certainly none of her business.

Certainly they seemed nicely matched in one respect, anyway, Kate found when she tried to foist off Robyn's offer to help with the dishes.

The effort was foiled in the same way Ben had handled it; Robyn had marched into the kitchen and was elbow-deep in the dishwater while Kate was still protesting.

The older woman kept up a running commentary throughout the cleaning up, and by the time they were finished Kate had discovered that Robyn was far more than just a housekeeper for her bachelor brother. She was widely travelled, had been a schoolteacher, a chef in several New Zealand restaurants and some in Europe as well, and had even, for a time, run a restaurant of her own.

And when Kate went over to help her unpack, while the two men relaxed over brandy and cigars in the lounge, it was to find that Robyn Campbell was a woman of style in every respect. Her clothes were tasteful and well chosen, and most showed the European influence from her travels.

There was little sophistication, however, when Robyn turned out in jeans and walking boots to join Kate on the fence patrol the next morning. She was, in her own words, 'always a country person at heart,' and she seemed to enjoy the stroll quite as much as Kate and the attendant donkeys.

The two women spent a good deal of time together in the next few days, finding a variety of common interests and quickly becoming firm friends. So firm, indeed, that when Robyn asked some rather pointed and personal questions on the morning of Ben Croft's expected return, Kate was able to take the questions in her stride.

Partly, of course, this was due to Robyn's delightfully straightforward and lighthearted approach to almost any situation.

'I suppose you just can't wait for Ben to get here,' she asked Kate, leaping into the inquisition without preamble. 'You're certain to be halfway in love with him, unless he's lost his touch or there's something dreadfully the matter with you.'

'Not halfway, but I'll admit to finding him moderately attractive,' Kate replied with a grin.

'Moderately attractive? He's absolutely gorgeous,' Robyn cooed. 'If I were a bit younger . . . Wow!' Which made Kate grin even more widely, knowing as she now did that Robyn was just forty, looked thirty, and couldn't even conceive of thinking that age made the slightest difference in man–woman affairs.

'At least you can get along with him,' she replied almost

ruefully. 'Every time I have anything to do with him, it ends in a squabble. I really don't think he likes me any better than I like him.'

'Liking means nothing,' Robyn declared. 'He likes me just fine, but it would never do me any good. Probably for the best, actually; we'd drive each other mad in a month.'

'I can't imagine why, from your point of view,' Kate said. 'I mean, he drives me mad in minutes, but you don't suffer from the same personality clash with him that I do.'

'No, but then I'm a quite different person from you. Ben says I talk too much, and of course he's right. But the point is that I *really* talk too much—for him. For me—he's simply much too strong a personality; I couldn't handle it.'

'I suppose you're trying to say he wants his women meek and submissive, as well as quiet,' Kate mused. 'No wonder we don't get along. My submissive days are over— for ever!'

Robyn laughed. 'Not if you get tangled up with Ben,' she chuckled. 'I wouldn't go so far as to say he demands meekness and outright submissiveness, but he's a winner, and he's one of the most dominating, domineering males I've ever met. He's not about to let any woman—or man— be the dominant one in a really personal relationship.'

'Well, neither am I, which solves that problem very nicely,' said Kate. 'And probably just as well, since I'm rather *off* men for the time being, and rather enjoying it.'

'Fool! When you're older, let's hope you'll realise there isn't much a man can do to you that a better one can't fix. If I were in your shoes, Kate, I'd be back at the house making damned sure it was *me* who got the treat of picking him up from the airport. And not dressed like that, either,' she continued with a scathing glance at Kate's worn jeans and shirt.

The whole comment was just too close to Kate's thinking, and so of course she rejected it hastily.

'No, thanks! I don't care about impressing him that way,' she lied. 'All I want to do is get by without a fight every time I encounter him. But you go, if you like. You've still time to change.'

'Not a chance,' Robyn scoffed. 'I've got my sights set on a far different target, and for once I'm not saying one more word about it. Might queer my luck.'

'Far be it from me to pry,' Kate replied, not bothering to hide her curiosity. 'Although they must be pretty long range sights to find a target from way out here. Or have you found some eligible type that I've missed?'

'The difference, my child, is in knowing where to look,' Robyn replied airily. 'If you can only barely see Ben Croft as eligible, your judgment is open to considerable question. For what it's worth, however, I'll tell you now that it's nobody that you and I are likely to be competing over, I hope.'

'So do I,' Kate laughed. 'Not that it would be much of a contest with your looks. Even in those clothes you make me feel positively dowdy!'

Robyn looked down at herself, seeing clothing almost identical to what Kate was wearing. 'Clothes don't make the woman, no matter what they say,' she replied. 'Besides, where Ben's concerned, it's a rather different type from me that you'll have to worry about. How are you with chopsticks and Oriental cooking?'

'Lousy,' Kate replied honestly. 'Although I really don't get your point.'

'Wait until the next velvet season and you will,' Robyn said. 'One of the top buyers out of Hong Kong has a sister who makes Suzie Wong look like a virgin schoolgirl. Her name, not that you'll ever mistake her for anyone else once

you've seen her, is Kim Lee, and she is the living proof
that Oriental women have something we just can't even
imagine.'

She breathed deeply and stared off into space for a
moment before continuing. 'She's about *this* high, with a
figure that combines everything a man could dream of,
she's beautiful, with hair so long she can sit on it, and—
worst of all—she's a witch!'

Kate laughed. 'Go on, next you'll be telling me she
enchants men by feeding them powdered deer horn.'

'Antler, dear,' Robyn corrected her. 'Deer have antlers,
not horns. And deer antler is *not* an aphrodisiac; for goodness' sake get that straight or you'll be in for a six-hour
lecture one day from Ben. Not to change the subject—
Kim Lee *is* a witch. She not only got my big brother Billy
talking, one day last year, she kept him talking for half an
hour! *That* is witchcraft, let me tell you. I think she's heard
more from him than I have in my whole life.'

The thought of taciturn, silent Bill Campbell being
charmed into speech by a diminutive Oriental beauty
caused Kate to erupt in spasms of giggling.

'Half an hour? She must have used something a lot
stronger than powdered deer . . . antlers.' Kate laughed.

'Oh, she did. Much stronger,' Robyn replied with unexpected seriousness. 'She used the strongest magic of all—
sex! And be warned, Kate, just in case you suddenly decide
Ben Croft is abundantly eligible after all. Kim Lee uses sex
like nobody I've ever seen in my life. No offence, but in a
head-on confrontation, you'd be a popgun against a nuc-
lear bomb.'

'I don't really think there's much chance of it,' Kate
replied evasively, hiding the involuntary shiver that sped
up her spine.

'Don't say it too lightly. Dear Ben has a habit of growing

on you. You might find that this time he's much more appealing than you thought,' Robyn replied.

She couldn't have been more right—or more wrong. Right, in that Ben *looked* even more impressive than usual when he slid from the passenger side of the Range Rover a few hours later, having been picked up at the airport by Bill Campbell. He was dressed casually in snug drill trousers and a shirt that was open halfway down the front to reveal the curling hair on his chest. He was tanned and healthy-looking, vital.

But his disposition, from Kate's viewpoint, left more to be desired than usual.

'I really would have expected *you* to pick me up, rather than take Bill away from his work,' he said without even the preamble of a good morning or how are you? or anything else.

'Well, *I* would have expected you to have arrived in a better mood,' Robyn interjected before Kate could stifle her own anger sufficiently to speak at all. 'You'll apologise to Kate this very minute or go without any of the lunch that we've spent all morning preparing in *your* honour. And what's more, I won't love you any more either.'

'We couldn't have that,' he replied blandly. 'It's bad enough the way Kate feels about me, without you turning against me as well. All right, I apologise, Kate. Although I really can't see that it should take two women all morning to make a simple lunch for five people.'

'If that's what you call an apology—forget it,' Kate snapped. 'And I hope you choke on your lunch, although I can't be bothered staying around to watch!'

And she turned on her heel and fled, forcing herself not to run as she stormed off through the deer yards to share her misery with the ever-tolerant donkeys.

'Damn you anyway, Ben Croft,' she muttered over and

over as she marched along. 'I really *do* hope you choke!'

The last was said quite loudly, and drew a most un-expected response. 'Well, if I do, at least I'll have the satisfaction of knowing you're there to watch,' came a harsh voice in her ear, and fingers like steel clamped on to her arm to halt her in her tracks.

She almost screamed in her surprise. Ben had material-ised as if from nowhere, stepping out from a shadowy corner of the high-boarded yards.

'Let me go, damn it! Where did you come from? Let go!' The words poured from her, but her attempts to free herself were ridiculously ineffectual.

'I designed these yards; I know all the short cuts,' he replied blithely. 'Has anybody ever told you that you must be the most short-tempered bitch in the world?'

He lithely dodged a kick that would have unmanned him had it landed, and merely laughed mockingly as Kate tried it again, and again failed.

'Keep that up and I'll start to think you're serious,' he sneered. 'You make it very difficult to apologise.'

'You had your chance to apologise,' Kate panted, still writhing in his immovable grip. 'And after what you said, I wouldn't accept an apology anyway. You're nothing but a stupid, arrogant male chauvinist pig! And I hate you!'

'That's a bit strong, but I'll put it down to your uncer-tain temper,' he retorted. 'Now settle down like a good little girl, and we'll stroll back quietly to enjoy that famous lunch.'

Kate's reply was vivid enough to bring a quick flush of anger to his face, but it was immediately replaced by a tautening of his jaw muscles and a cruel sneer. 'And I can do without that kind of language,' he growled. 'Now stop it!'

Kate's response was drawn from the depths of Wayne's

vocabulary, and she spat out the words like an angry cat. It was brutally graphic, and Ben's response equally brutal.

A flick of his wrist sent her crashing against the yard hoardings, and she struck so hard that half the breath was driven from her lungs. Before she could replace it she was yanked forward again, this time to land unceremoniously across Ben's knees as he sat himself in the dirt, dragging her down with him.

'All right, missy, you asked for this,' he muttered, 'and just be glad I haven't any soapy water handy, or you'd get your mouth washed out as well!'

The first stinging blow to Kate's upturned rear was more humiliating than painful; the ones that followed quickly had her writhing in anger, then agony. And still he continued. And continued.

'Now then, are you going to promise to act like a lady, or do you want some more?' he demanded. Kate, her bottom on fire and her vision blurred by tears of pain and rage, snarled a vitriolic reply that turned to a shriek as he spanked her again.

'My hand will last longer than your rump,' he grunted. 'Want to change your mind?'

'I'll . . . kill . . . you,' she gasped.

'Very likely,' he sighed. 'But you'll clean up your language first, I promise you that.' And he spanked her twice more with incredible force but somehow, Kate thought, less enthusiasm. Perhaps it was only that she was becoming numb from the assault. She renewed her futile struggle to escape.

'Will you hurry up and apologise? My hand's getting sore,' he snarled, and the incongruity of the remark would have made Kate laugh if she hadn't been so close to giving in. It did, however, renew her determination.

Unfortunately, it seemed that Ben's determination was

equally strong, and his ingenuity was stronger yet.

'You've either got a cast-iron rump, or it's these jeans,' he muttered half to himself. Then, before Kate could comprehend the remark, he was reaching for the side zipper, rasping it open in one easy movement, and to her astonishment began to peel the trousers from her.

'No!' she squealed. 'Oh . . . no! No. I . . . I'll apologise. You stop that!'

Which, surprisingly, he did. But only for a moment, in which Kate was too winded to speak. And because she didn't—couldn't—say anything, he took her silence for a new refusal and tugged at the jeans once more.

'No!' she gasped. 'I apologise.' And he stopped again.

'Do you?' he asked brightly. To which all Kate could do was nod.

'Excellent!' he mused in supercilious tones. 'So now you will repeat after me . . . I hereby promise on my honour to stop using naughty language, and to behave like a lady at all times, but especially those times when Benton Croft is present.'

Kate nearly choked on the words, but she got them out and then started twisting free of his grasp, hoping her humiliation was finally ended.

His grip on her merely tightened, however, and a light tap to her burning bottom reminded her that he wasn't yet done.

'And . . .' he continued blithely, 'that I shall from now on cease treating the aforesaid Benton Croft like some kind of ogre, knowing as I do that it upsets him, and that it would also upset my father.'

'Like hell!' she snapped, and squealed as his broad palm smacked down like thunder on a bottom no longer protected except for the skimpiness of her panties.

'Ah, much better,' he crooned—and then laughed a

horrid, evil, mocking laughter that sent shivers down Kate's spine. She was totally helpless. One huge hand held her by the back of the neck, and he had her legs pinioned with one of his own so that she hadn't a hope of freeing herself.

There was no one to see, no one within hearing. He was free to paddle her until she was black and blue, or ... Kate shivered as his fingers suddenly touched her again, not spanking this time, but caressing the base of her spine with an infinite, soothing tenderness.

And his voice, when he spoke, had lost its harshness, become almost melodious. '. . . so stubborn you'd probably let yourself be beaten senseless, but there's more than one way to skin a cat.'

The hand at her neck shifted, somehow, and before Kate quite realised what was happening she had been turned so she was cradled in his arms, and his lips were bruising against hers as he used his mouth to continue her punishment.

Her breasts were crushed against his muscular chest, and the heat of their bodies mingled through the thin material of their shirts. The sudden switch of tactics defeated Kate entirely; her body betrayed her from the instant his lips met hers, and her mouth softened to meet his lips, to merge with them.

Her hands, no longer pinioned, crept up along his shoulders to twine in the thick hair at the back of his neck, and his own hands were free then to explore the contours of her with expert skill.

He touched her throat, her cheek, and then his fingers moved down her throat to the open neckline of her shirt. And after an instant, his lips followed, only to return just in time to stifle her soft moan of protest. His fingers stroked and caressed the soft hollow at the base of her spine, bringing waves of ecstasy through her before shifting to coax further waves from her turgid nipples.

Kate was lost. Nothing in her experience had ever prepared her for the sheer, mindless intensity of her own physical reaction, for the impact of such awesome masculinity. Her entire body was alive, singing a wanton song of submission as those incredible fingers moved down to where the sheerness of her panties was a final, futile defence.

She twisted herself, fitting herself closer, using her fingers, her lips, her body to bring him ever nearer, to unite them in a fulfilment of the throbbing desires within her.

His fingers were a cool balm as they traced idle and erotic patterns across the burning sensitivity of her bottom, and the scent of him was a heady, rousing tang in her nostrils.

'My God!' he whispered, and his voice was a gentle, sighing windsong. But his fingers moved away, sliding up to cradle her back as he slowly, delicately muted the intensity of their lovemaking, bringing Kate ever so slowly back to the reality of where they were and what they were doing.

'My God!' Her own voice, this time, voicing the total incredulity of it all, the fantasy-like almost-reality of having surrendered herself so joyfully to this man—in the cool darkness of an animal loading yard.

She looked at him, finally, having steeled herself for the ultimate degradation, the rejection she knew must come with the return of reality. But his eyes were merely perplexed, and gentle.

He slid her from his lap, rising to his feet and helping her up, steadying her as she fumbled to fasten her jeans and straighten her shirt.

Kate was numb. All of her, that was, but the flaming,

now-tender reminder of how it had begun. Her mind was a riot of impressions, of reflections, of sensations so incredibly vivid they frightened her. She looked up at Ben Croft again, her eyes wide, and he leaned down to kiss her gently on the lips.

'I'll never try to spank *you* again,' he whispered. 'I don't know who won that encounter, but I know that I very nearly lost. Forgive me, Kate, if you can manage it.'

And before she could reply, he turned her gently around and steered her back towards the house. Kate stumbled forward, stepping unevenly at first and then settling into a slow, steady pace that matched the bewilderment in her mind. The pace of a zombie, she thought. And if he very nearly lost, what did *I* do?

She was no closer to an answer half an hour later, having showered and changed to a light summer frock before joining Robyn in the final preparations involving luncheon. The older woman's knowing looks didn't help a great deal either.

'I gather you and Ben have . . . er . . . made up your little squabble,' Robyn said, her eyes focussing on Kate's swollen lips and still-high colour.

Made up? Kate had to stifle what would have emerged as an hysterical giggle. If that was making up, what would happen after a serious, *really* serious fight? she wondered.

The lack of an answer didn't upset Robyn at all; neither did it stifle her curiosity. She flooded Kate with a barrage of questions, ignoring the fact that Kate didn't answer her, and gradually made up a surprisingly accurate account of what had happened.

'It's obvious,' she replied to Kate's unasked question. 'You have the look, my child, of a woman who's been very, very thoroughly kissed. And enjoyed it! Not that you'd admit that, of course.'

Hardly pausing for a breath, and totally ignoring Kate's indrawn breath and growing frustration with the verbal assault, she continued, 'But you can't fool me, Kate. You may be able to continue telling yourself that you don't fancy dear Ben, but don't try it while looking in the mirror.'

Kate fought back a bitter, angry retort. It was only Robyn's way, she thought, but how she wished the woman would shut up! It was bad enough having to face reality by herself, without listening to the running commentary at the same time.

'Please, Robyn, just drop it, will you?' she pleaded. 'Sometimes you really do talk too much.'

'All right, dear,' Robyn replied, not at all offended. 'Anyway, it's time to feed the starving hordes, so will you take in the ducklings and I'll bring the veggies?'

The three men, all scrubbed and tidy for their meal, brightened visibly when Kate emerged from the kitchen bearing a huge tray of succulent, plump young ducklings—one for each diner.

'Now that,' quipped Ben, 'is what I call a proper lunch. I'm surprised you get any work done here at all, if this is any example of the tucker. I may have to settle down here permanently.'

'You wouldn't get meals like this then,' Robyn said. 'We only provide such luxury for important visitors, and you wouldn't qualify as a permanent resident. Besides, you haven't tasted it yet.'

'If you cooked it, Robyn, I have no doubt whatsoever that it will taste as good as it looks,' he replied seriously.

'Ah, but I didn't,' she retorted. 'This is almost entirely Kate's work.' Which was really stretching the truth a very great deal, since she'd supervised everything, and Kate deliberately turned away to hide her confusion at such a deliberately misleading statement.

But when she turned back again, eyes showing mild surprise at the silence, she found Ben waiting to capture her with a direct stare. 'That's even better,' he said very quietly, and she dropped her eyes from the frank pleasure she read in his glance.

Hardly had the meal begun before Kate was regretting her decision to sit almost directly opposite Ben's place at table. It had been an instinctive bid to keep her from being too close, where the very nearness of him would have been, she was sure, impossible to ignore. But being across from him was worse.

He said little during the meal, leaving Robyn to carry the conversational ball with occasional passes to Kate's father. But, it seemed, every time Kate glanced up it was to find Ben regarding her appraisingly. At the very least, she thought, he didn't exhibit that horrid, *I have conquered* look, but then Ben Croft wasn't the type to have to shout his conquests to the world. He knew, and she knew; that was more than enough.

Lost in her own thoughts, Kate was only partially following the conversation, and she didn't catch the point at which it switched to antler velvet and the Russian influence on markets. It wasn't until Ben's voice joined in that she tuned back in, to hear him say he'd be going overseas fairly soon to try and determine next season's demand and prices.

'Did you know, Kate, that they raise large herds of deer in China and Russia exclusively for their antlers?' Robyn asked.

'Of course the Orientals all deny that it's powdered into some form of aphrodisiac, but I'm not convinced.' She turned to Ben, then, but not for confirmation of her theory.

'Did you ever ask that little Chinese fortune cookie who
follows you around every time her brother comes to buy
velvet? Oh, what's her name? But you know who I mean,
Ben. The way she used to look at you, I reckoned her
brother was buying the velvet just for her . . .' She broke
off as Ben's eyes turned to the flat, polished green of jade
and his voice broke into her monologue.

Softly, dangerously calm, Kate thought, he replied,
'Robyn, has anybody ever told you that you talk too
damned much?'

'Oh,' said Robyn with a cat-that-swallowed-the-canary
smirk. 'Oh yes—frequently!' And the glance she shot in
Kate's direction spoke volumes.

'Her name is Kim Lee,' Bill Campbell interjected, and
Kate winced at the inappropriate timing of the remark.

Bad enough, she thought, that normally every single
word had to be dragged physically from the crusty old
bachelor's mouth. But this time, his total insensitivity to
the growing tension could be the crowning touch.

But Ben, surprisingly, had regained his humour instantly. 'And she's Eurasian, as you very well know,
Robyn,' he added. 'And, since she's a very well qualified
doctor, I'm sure she'd be the first to tell you that antler
velvet is used purely for medicinal purposes. So stop
peddling archaic Western rumours, would you?'

Robyn, having satisfied her desire to make him squirm
just a little, or at least to probe deliberately into his usually-
hidden feelings, only grinned.

'Of course, Ben,' she cooed. 'And you don't have to
get all serious about a simple dinner-table conversation. After all, it isn't as if I'd accused you of trying it
yourself!'

Ben's wry grin was her only answer, and Kate breathed
an inner sigh of relief. The angry confrontation she

had feared was over.

Not quite! 'Well,' Robyn urged, having set the scene and been temporarily slowed by his silence, 'have you?'

Ben's generous mouth quirked slightly, and his eyes, when he finally answered, shot to Kate, not to Robyn.

'Some of us,' he said very deliberately, 'don't need any artificial stimulants.' And there was no anger in his eyes, only a slight, unmistakable mockery.

Mockery, Kate thought, and something else. An awareness, a speculativeness, and a warning. A warning that said clearer than words, 'You've been discussing our personal affairs with Robyn and I don't like it.'

But I haven't, she thought, almost speaking the words aloud. Only it was already too late, because Ben was shoving back his chair and suggesting to her father and Bill that they could have their coffee in the office, since there was much to be done and he had to be leaving first thing next morning.

'And that's a lot of bunk,' Robyn told Kate as soon as they were safely out of earshot in the kitchen. 'He brought enough gear to stay for a week at least. I think you're getting to him, Kate. He turned positively livid when I mentioned his little Oriental friend.'

'Oh, Robyn, it isn't me that's getting to him,' Kate cried in exasperation. 'Don't you see that it's your constant stirring that's got to him? He couldn't care less about me, one way or another. And frankly, the feeling's mutual.'

'You're a poor liar, Kate,' Robyn replied cheerfully. 'And, I might also point out, don't teach your grandmother to suck eggs. Ben probably will leave tomorrow. But he'll be back, and *then* is what we've got to be prepared for. I think we'll have to find you a boy-friend; that'll get him going and keep him going.'

'No . . . a thousand times no,' Kate objected, knowing

deep inside that Robyn would neither listen nor heed. 'I'll
have nothing to do with your schemes, so just forget it.'

'Oh, stop being so melodramatic,' Robyn replied
haughtily. 'We're not exactly *scheming*; just sort of laying
the groundwork for later. And besides, all's fair in love and
war.'

'Well, maybe from your viewpoint, but not from mine,'
Kate said firmly. 'You didn't see the look he gave me
when you began mouthing off at lunch. If he thought you
and I . . .'

'Now why would I think anything like that?' drawled a
sarcastic voice from the doorway behind them. 'Not that
anything Robyn gets involved in would surprise me—not
one little bit. But you, Kate, I'd expect to have more
sense.'

Kate was stunned into silence. Stunned, and more; she
was mortified. How much had he heard? And even if it
were only her last remark, what horrid context could he
create for it? As if there were one more horrid than the
truth.

Robyn had no such problem. 'You shouldn't eavesdrop
and expect to hear well of yourself. Eavesdroppers never
do,' she told Ben chillingly.

'I didn't hear anything about myself,' he replied with
maddening calm. 'Not that it would matter; I've been
called worse things in worse places, I'm sure. What interests me is what kind of scheme you two are hatching.
Surely you're not deliberately enlisting Kate's help in a
scheme to trap old Henry, or are you, Robyn?'

Kate couldn't believe her ears. Then she glanced over
at Robyn and could less believe her eyes. Had Ben Croft
struck a tender nerve? Certainly he'd done something;
Robyn was white as a sheet, and, for once, dumbstruck.

'That was an incredibly horrid and crude thing to say,'

Kate snapped, leaping to her friend's defence without really being sure why. 'You must have led an awful life if that's the kind of thing you automatically infer from a conversation you had no business listening to in the first place!'

'Let's just say that I've learned over the years to be wary when women begin plotting,' he replied calmly. And to Kate's surprise, he walked over to clasp Robyn by the shoulders and kiss her gently on the forehead.

'Sorry, Rob. I didn't realise I was so close to the mark or I'd have kept my big mouth shut,' he said softly. 'I think you'd probably both be very good for each other, and when Kate gets over being shirty with me, I'm sure she'll agree.'

Robyn said nothing, but her great eyes pooled with unspilled tears, and she looked to Kate as if pleading for understanding and compassion.

'My God!' Kate thought half aloud. Ben had been closer to the mark than even *he* realised. And clearly it was now up to her to extricate both herself and Robin from this unexpected development.

'Personally, I think you're being ridiculous, Ben Croft,' she snapped. 'But if you're so positive you know everything, let me just tell you that I couldn't be happier if Robyn and my father got together. It would certainly show that his taste in women was better than his taste in so-called friends!'

Either Kate's blistering attack, or perhaps merely the recovery time it afforded, gave Robyn a chance to at least partially regain her composure.

Shoving Ben away with a scornful gesture, she turned on both of them. 'I really think both of you have got a quite ridiculous bee in your bonnets,' she scoffed. 'Really! I mean, I've only been here a few days, and to think . . . to think . . . oh, hell! It's nothing but a load of rubbish!' And she spun away out of the room, leaving neither remaining party any further doubts about her thoughts.

'You really should be ashamed of yourself,' Kate snarled, her eyes blazing with emotion. 'Of all the crude, heavy-handed, insensitive things I've ever seen in my life . . .'

'Oh, shut up! There's been quite enough said already,' he retorted, obviously as angry with himself as was Kate. 'I'm just as sorry as you are, but it's out now, and it's up to us, dear Kate, to make damned sure that it never goes any farther. Except of its own accord, that is. Personally, I couldn't be more delighted if it does happen. Robyn's a marvellous girl; I'd marry her myself if we weren't such good friends.'

'Well, she'd have to be a fool to have you,' Kate replied sulkily. 'As a friend, you make an admirable enemy.'

'Admirable? My goodness, Kate, you're slipping,' Ben replied with a slow grin. 'I wouldn't have thought you'd find anything about me admirable . . . or did this morning change your mind?'

'All this morning did was prove that you're a healthy male animal and I'm not as dead from the neck down as you obviously thought,' she retorted. 'Any young stud with the right equipment could have done as well.'

'So speaks the voice of experience, I suppose,' he replied, eyes dark with barely-suppressed anger. 'Is that how your husband died—chasing around trying to keep track of your extra-curricular activities?'

Kate blanched, unable to find any reply to his horridly inaccurate charge. Her hand flashed up like a striking snake, smashing against his cheek so hard that she recoiled with the pain of it.

'You . . . bastard!' she hissed. 'You insufferable bastard!'

Ben said nothing; he stood rigid as a statue with the

brand of her slap spreading slowly across his cheek and his glittering eyes alive with hellish green fury.

Kate backed away from those eyes, slowly moving until she collided with the kitchen counter. Her blind, searching hand scrabbled behind her, searching for any possible weapon. And finding one in the form of the big kitchen carving knife.

Wielding it like a sword, she crouched to face the still unmoving man, the man whose eyes promised a fate too horrible for her even to comprehend.

'Get out!' she cried. 'Get out, or by all that's holy I'll use this on you!'

Then, in total silence, they stood and stared at each other, until finally he flexed his shoulders idly, and spoke.

'Don't bother,' he sneered, and every twist of his mouth carried the same anger and disgust as his eyes. He snorted, as if trying to clear his flaring nostrils of a particularly offensive smell, then turned and stalked from the room.

Kate stayed where she was, unable to move lest her knees cave in, until her consciously slowed breathing allowed her to dare to straighten up and fling the carving knife into the sink. She was standing, staring down into the soapy water and trying to stop trembling, when her father entered the kitchen.

'Where's Ben?' he queried. 'He said he was coming out to ask for more coffee.' Then he caught the expression on his daughter's face.

'My God, Kate, what's wrong?' He stepped forward, alert with concern, but Kate shook her head and managed a wan smile.

'It's all right, Dad. I . . . I just about took off a finger with the carving knife, that's all. Scared myself silly—and for nothing, because there isn't even a cut.'

It was a lame excuse, but for some reason it satisfied

him, and Kate was able to shoo him away again after promising to bring some fresh coffee in just a few minutes.

It took all her determination to enter the small office with a tray of coffee and biscuits in trembling fingers. But Ben didn't so much as glance up, though he murmured his thanks along with the other two men.

Kate returned to the kitchen and spent some time in venting her anger and frustration on the dirty dishes. Then, as she began the preliminary plans for that evening's dinner, she began to find concentration almost impossible.

Her mind swung back and forth like a mad pendulum, first encompassing the not-so-incredible possibility of a relationship between Robyn and Kate's father, then to the less pleasurable components of Kate's own relationship—if it might be truly called that—with Ben Croft.

At the very least, she determined, his comments about her 'extra-curricular activities' had revealed his true feelings, and had also clarified his actions earlier that day.

'Damn!' she muttered, unable to forestall the bitter taste that seeped into her mouth at the very thought of their final verbal battle.

How *could* he think such thing? And why? Surely she'd given him no real reason for it, even considering her admittedly wanton behaviour in the deer yards.

Thoughts of *that*, unfortunately, mingled chagrin with tormenting remembrances—purely physical ones, she assured herself—with the resultant blend most difficult to assess.

She couldn't deny her responses to Ben's artful caresses, but she was both repulsed and intrigued by the sudden shift from pain to passion as he had first spanked her and then made love to her as it had never been done before. Compared to Ben Croft, husband Wayne had been a rank, fumbling amateur; no wonder he'd been wont to prey on young, innocent girls who couldn't recognise his ineptness, even as Kate hadn't.

She spent most of the afternoon frankly hiding in her room, trying to read and failing, trying to think and doing little better. At one point she considered wandering over to the cottage, but then wisely reconsidered with the correct assumption that Robyn would be happier alone with her own thoughts.

At dinner, both Kate and Robyn were subdued, though the older woman had regained most of her composure and could face both Kate and Ben without a tremor. But it was left to Henry Lyle and Ben to carry the conversation—rather a change from lunch—and Kate found Ben's broad-handed conviviality frankly repugnant.

It seemed gross and hypocritical for him to keep trying to draw her into conversation, especially when it was all she could do to avoid snapping at his every overture. Arrogant beast! Yet she returned him grudging smile for grudging smile, and took immense pleasure in knowing that he was enjoying the evening no more than she.

And she was especially soppy-sweet when she enquired at one point how long he would be staying this time.

'Here's your hat—what's your hurry?' he countered with grim humour in his eyes. 'Well, Kate, I know you'd love me to stay longer, and your cooking is a great temptation. But I'm forced to leave first thing tomorrow.'

Which was not surprising, but a good deal more pleasant than his immediate insistence that it should be Kate who drove him to the airport.

CHAPTER FIVE

'Is there some particular reason why you insisted on me playing chauffeur?' she snarled when they were finally alone together in the car and she could throw off the hypocritical pretence that had made breakfast a nightmare.

'Obviously I wanted the pleasure of your scintillating company,' he replied with equal venom. 'Although just exactly why, I can't imagine.'

'Well, neither can I,' Kate replied honestly enough, crashing through the gears as she sped towards the gate. Once there, Ben stepped from the car, opened the gate, and held it until she had driven through. Only this time there was none of the gallantry he had displayed on their first meeting.

When he returned, she couldn't help but notice the determined set of his jaw, and the fact that he kept his eyes straight ahead and his mouth shut as she drove down the road.

She too was silent, having nothing to say that wasn't best avoided, and it wasn't until they were almost at Mapleton that the silence was broken.

'I'm sorry about yesterday,' said Ben, biting off the ambiguous statement abruptly.

'Which part?' Kate asked snappily, 'the almost roll in the hay, or calling me a whore afterwards?' The words seemed to form themselves, frothing out with all the bitterness she felt inside.

Ben's face took on a stoic rigidity. 'The latter, obviously,' he replied after a moment. 'I'm not going to apologise for the lovemaking, which I'm sure you enjoyed as much as I did. Although,' he mused, 'I suppose I did get a bit carried away with the spanking bit.'

Kate, whose bottom still registered the effects, couldn't but agree. 'You certainly did,' she replied. 'Although it's no more than I've come to expect from you.'

His chuckle was frigid. 'You seem to have come to expect some pretty awful things from me, haven't you, Kate? Although I must say you give as good as you get.'

Kate didn't bother to reply, her attention split between his words and the exceptionally tricky bit of road ahead of her. She sensed, rather than saw, Ben Croft looking at her, but he too stayed silent until the worst of the twisty section was past.

'Seriously, Kate,' he said then, 'I don't understand this amazing bitterness you always exhibit. I'm not especially noted for instilling bitterness in people.'

'Undoubtedly because of your astounding modesty,' she replied sarcastically. 'But if it will ease your conscience—presuming you have one—I'm not bitter, as you put it, towards you. I don't like you. I think you're arrogant and overbearing and cruel, and I could quite cheerfully do without your company. But bitter? No!'

'Well, you won't have much of my company during the next few months. That should please you.'

'Immensely. Although I'm sure you won't be staying away just to please me.'

His laugh was harsh. 'And you claim you're not bitter? My God, woman—listen to yourself! Is it just me, I wonder, or are you just off men in general?'

'Both, actually,' Kate replied grimly. 'Although you'd be enough, just by yourself, to put any woman off men for life.'

'Ouch! You really do have a low opinion of me, don't

you? Strange, that . . . because I rather like you, at least most of the time.'

What could she say to that? It was hardly the line she might have expected him to take, and for a moment it threw her totally off balance.

Ben Croft saw that, and took full advantage of her confusion. 'Ah, didn't expect that, did you? Or is it that you've so little confidence in yourself that you have to be over-defensive? Somehow I get the feeling you're not really the grieving widow you make out.'

That was simply too close to the truth. But before she could formulate a reply, he continued his verbal attack.

'Is that it, Kate? Nobody as happily married as you insist you were could have such a cynical attitude towards marriage, although you put on a damned good act when your father's handy, I'll give you that. What I can't figure out is why . . . because he'd be the first person to under-stand if your marriage wasn't working out. He never expected it to, and I'm sure you know that.'

All too well, Kate thought, aghast at the possibility that her father would have been guilty of discussing her mar-riage with this . . . this frustrating man. In her short time at Kathryn Downs, she'd already brought her father round to an acceptance that the past was not for discussion, but it seemed that Ben Croft had no such injunction in his own mind.

'Personally,' she replied with infinite, careful coolness, 'I don't think it's any of your business. If you want to discuss marriage all that badly, go and find a wife and discuss your own.'

'What? And deny myself the pleasure of finding out what makes my Katie tick?' His chuckle was positively devilish.

'I'm not *your* Katie or anybody else's!' she snapped peevishly. 'And if you can't find something else to talk about, then please just shut up.'

'Temper, temper,' he chided. 'For all you know, I am considering taking a wife. Maybe even you—but you couldn't expect me to give you serious consideration without knowing your track record.'

'And don't be absurd,' Kate snapped, refusing even to remotely consider that he might be serious. Why couldn't the man shut up? Or did he get some truly sadistic pleasure out of probing at her?

'What's absurd about it? You're of suitable age; you're remarkably pretty when you try to be; you're rather personable, with everybody but me. You're also an excellent cook, which counts for a great deal.' He paused, then, provocatively. 'And we already know that we're quite well suited physically. Even you can't deny that.'

A torrent of abuse flooded into Kate's mind, but she kept her eyes on the road and her mouth shut. 'Damn him!' she muttered inside her throat. Damn, and double-damn. Well, she could play at that game too. And win, provided she could hold her temper.

'What? Nothing to say? That's not like you, Kate. One of the things I've come to look forward to is your ready tongue and sparkling wit. Come on, let's have your honest opinion.'

'And risk another spanking? No, thank you,' she replied with feigned gentleness.

'Oh, you're quite safe there. My hand's still sore from last time,' he grinned. And then, in a rather startling change of direction, 'Okay, let's talk about your dad and Robyn instead. Does your cynicism about marriage apply to them as well?'

'I am not cynical about marriage,' Kate snapped. 'And whatever Dad and Robyn do is none of my business.

Despite your attempts to fit me into the role, I am not my father's keeper.'

'But you are his daughter. Surely you have some interest in his future romantic liaisons. Or do you really not care?'

'Of course I care! But it really is his business. If he and Robyn get something going, it's their affair. They don't need me getting involved—or you either!'

'Since I'm not going to be there, I'm hardly likely to become involved,' Ben replied thoughtfully. 'But it mightn't be quite so easy for you.'

'It will be very easy,' Kate said. And with the words, a sudden but eminently logical decision. 'Because I shan't be there either, or at least not that often.'

'What?' His disbelief was a balm to Kate's shattered feelings. Hah! she thought. Got you there, didn't I? And she grinned smugly as she waited for what must come.

'You'd best explain that,' he said, in a voice that was grimly serious.

'I don't see why,' she retorted lightly.

'Well, I do! Or have you forgotten that one of the basic reasons for you being here is to keep an eye on your father?'

'One of *your* basic reasons,' she replied. 'My intent was only to get a bit closer than I was in Melbourne. Besides, with Bill Campbell on the spot, there's no longer any danger of Dad overworking himself, and Robyn surely can manage to keep both of them fed and watered without my help.'

'Very likely,' Ben agreed surprisingly. 'But then what are you going to do—admitting as I ask that it's none of my business?'

'Exactly! But since you've asked, for once, I'll tell you what I'm going to do. I'm going to get rid of some excess and unwanted baggage at the airport, and then I'm going to look around Nambour and see if there's a job going that suits me.'

There was a long silence, and Kate risked a look with every expectation that she'd see only anger. Instead, Ben merely looked thoughtful.

'I don't suppose you'd change your mind, or at least put it off for a bit,' he ventured.

'I don't see why I should.'

'Well, one reason could be that you're in need of a good rest yourself,' he said, 'although I must admit you look a great deal better than when you arrived.'

'Well, thank you very much,' she replied tartly.

'You're quite welcome.' Sarcasm dripped from his voice. 'But I'm not at all certain you've fully recovered from the ordeal of . . . your husband's death, much less the obvious readjustments to your life-style. A couple of months without any new hassles would do you the world of good.'

'Might I remind you that it's been nearly four months since . . . then,' she retorted indignantly. 'Do you expect me to be overcome by . . . grief for ever?'

'That might depend on how much you really loved your husband,' said Ben with startling candour. 'Your father, though you might not realise it, is still making adjustments from your mother's death.'

'My father,' Kate replied acidly, 'was married for a great deal longer than I was.'

'He also knew your mother was going to die, and therefore had that much more warning that readjustments would be required,' Ben pointed out.

'Oh, for God's sake stop it!' Kate snapped, thoroughly fed up with the entire discussion. 'I'll adjust my own way and in my own time. And without any so-called help from you. If I want to look for a job, I'll do it, and if I find one that suits me, I'll take it. So if you don't like it, just go and stuff it up your jumper . . . is that clear?'

'Infinitely,' he replied. 'But take my advice whether you like it or not and have a bit more rest first. Your nerves are ragged as hell.'

'No thanks to you!' Kate snarled sulkily, then sighed with relief as the airport hove into view. Finally, thank heaven, she'd be able to rid herself of this infuriating passenger.

But when they reached the airport parking lot, Ben made no move to speed his departure. Instead, he lit a cigarette and leaned back in his seat, regarding her soberly through the smoke haze.

'You *are* coming in to see me off,' he said, making it more a statement than a question.

'If only to be sure you're really going,' she retorted. 'Shall we go? I feel the need of some fresh air.' Which wasn't totally true; she really only wanted to get him to where the presence of other people might keep him from continuing the inquisition.

'All right,' he shrugged, and slid out to collect his luggage and stalk beside her into the terminal building.

The southbound aircraft arrived a few minutes later, after Ben had checked his luggage, and he was standing with Kate at the terminal entrance, about to say goodbye, when a lilting, musical voice cried out his name.

'Ben . . . ton!' The voice broke up the name into two distinct parts, and Ben turned with a quick smile of recognition. *Pleased* recognition, Kate noted without any pleasure herself.

'Well, this is a surprise,' he laughed, opening his arms to receive a tidy little bundle of Oriental loveliness that seemed to fly at him from halfway across the terminal. Ruby lips joined with his in an impassioned kiss, but throughout the kiss the woman's eyes were fixed cat-like on Kate. And they were cold.

'A surprise?' she asked brightly when the long kiss was ended. 'You mean you did not come to meet us?'

'Pretty hard, when I didn't know you were coming,' he replied.

'Oh, but didn't your office call you?' she pouted prettily. 'They told us when we rang from Townsville that you were here, and promised to relay a message.'

'Must have been after we'd already left the station,' Ben replied. 'And I'm forgetting my manners. Kate, this is Kim Lee, and,' with a wave to where a tall young Oriental was now approaching with outstretched hand, 'her brother Ken, who's the canniest velver buyer in all Asia. Kate is Henry Lyle's daughter, come to help us run Kathryn Downs.'

Ken Lee reached out to take Kate's hand, murmuring a soft greeting with a genuine smile. His sister was less effusive.

'I see,' she said, making no attempt to greet Kate. 'But,' she turned to Ben immediately, 'if you are not here to meet us, then . . .?'

'I'm here to catch that plane back to Brisbane,' he replied, 'so if you're coming along, you'd best rearrange your plans.'

'Oh, yes,' she replied, and directed her brother in a rapid patter of what Kate presumed must be Chinese. Ken Lee shook his head, looking for all the world like a hen-pecked husband as he scurried away to carry out the instructions.

Kim slung her arm possessively through Ben's, thrusting her slim, lovely body against him as she cooed up at him with no regard whatsoever for Kate's presence.

'But why are you going back so soon?' she queried. 'They said at your office that you had planned a week here. Is there something wrong that you go away now so soon?'

His enigmatic glance took in Kate, but he merely said, 'I don't tell my office everything. Now let's get going before we miss the plane.'

Kim turned away, obviously planning to leave without a word, but her movement allowed Ben to free himself from her caressing grasp. Before Kate could react, he had taken her firmly by the shoulders and planted a slow, caressing kiss on her startled lips.

'Goodbye for now, Kate,' he said with a grin. 'See you next trip, and I hope I'll be able to stay longer next time.'

He walked away without a backward glance, leaving Kate standing with one hand lifted to her mouth. Kim Lee, however, after firmly grasping his arm as if to reaffirm her claim, shot back a glance from eyes like black ice. It was a look of pure, undiluted venom, so malignant that Kate shivered inside when thinking of it later.

For the moment, however, she merely stood watching as the tall, masculine figure with the voluptuous Asian doll beside him strode towards the waiting plane. Her attention was so locked, indeed, that she started with surprise when a soft voice beside her said, 'Miss Lyle? I am sorry we meet under such hurried circumstances. Surely we shall meet again?'

Ken Lee! 'Oh ... oh yes,' she stammered. 'I hope so too.' Whereupon he bowed slightly and trotted off to ensure that he, too, caught the waiting aircraft.

Kate watched until the plane lifted off and circled towards Brisbane, then slowly walked back to her car and drove almost as slowly back towards Nambour.

So that, she mused, was the infamous Kim Lee. It wasn't difficult to understand Robyn's comments, having now seen the Oriental sexpot in the flesh. The classic concubine,

Kate thought, combining beauty with a calculated sexiness that surely no Western woman could match.

And those eyes! Deadly, when looking at Kate herself, yet a man could drown in those eyes, swirling into a whirlpool of sensuality.

Her brother had seemed very nice, though. That rather old-fashioned dignity and soft manner was a pleasant change from the abruptness she had come to expect from Ben Croft.

Ben Croft . . . a man who had such incredible power to make Kate lose her temper—and her inhibitions. But an increasingly strange man, she thought, and wondered idly about his abrupt change in plans. Judging from Kim Lee's comments and Robyn's earlier remarks, it seemed certain that he had originally intended to stay more than just the one day. But he hadn't, and Kate wondered why. She knew very well he'd been in touch with his office the afternoon before, but if there was a pressing reason for his change of plans, he'd not mentioned it in her hearing, at least.

It was his final gesture, however, that totally unexpected kiss and the comments following it, which took most of Kate's introspection.

What on earth had he been thinking of? Certainly he hadn't hoped to impress Kate herself, except perhaps by incurring her wrath yet again. Ignoring, of course, the fact that she hadn't been angry at all. Had he simply been amusing himself . . . doing a final bit of point-scoring? That explanation didn't quite satisfy her.

Or had he, with some perverted logic, been deliberately ticking off his Oriental lover? Lover! Kate's stomach flipped even at the thought of Ben Croft being physically involved with such a blatantly sexual creature.

She was honest enough to view herself as no great threat

to Kim Lee's Oriental loveliness. Indeed it seemed ludicrous that Ben would have thought a mere kiss might cast doubts on Kim Lee's security of tenure. But then why that black-eyed look of malevolence? Could it be that Kim Lee wasn't all that sure of her position?

'Well, none of my affair anyway,' Kate told herself resolutely. 'She can have him and welcome, as far as I'm concerned.'

She arrived back in Nambour just in time for lunch, and splurged on a three-course seafood luncheon, complete with wine, at one of the town's better restaurants. It took some convincing to make herself believe that she was getting more pleasure from her lonely luncheon than Kim Lee would get from sharing dinner that evening with Ben Croft, as would surely be the case.

At least, Kate thought after becoming increasingly aware of several complimentary glances from businessmen sharing the restaurant, she still had some allure for the opposite sex.

The tangerine pants-suit she'd selected for her expedition lent extra colour to her skin and eyes, and the peasant neckline softened the harsh planes of her still-too-thin features.

I wonder how Ben Croft would view me in the face of all this attention? she wondered, coyly turning away from the direct, speculating stare of one especially brave diner who had been deliberately staring at her ever since he entered.

It wasn't until she got up to pay her bill and leave the restaurant that Kate suddenly realised it was the first time in two years that she had consciously been aware of—and even deliberately courted—the attentions of the opposite sex. Not counting, of course, her encounters with Ben Croft. Those, she decided, might have been blatantly sexual, but hardly romantic.

Only it was Ben Croft who dominated her thoughts as she finally steered for home, and she was halfway back to Kathryn Downs when she realised she had entirely forgotten her promise to find a job.

'Just as well, I suppose,' she mused. Certainly it would be more diplomatic to sound out her father on such a proposal before making a positive move, and besides, she hadn't the faintest idea what opportunities Nambour might offer.

There wasn't a university, as such, although she vaguely remembered that Nambour boasted a College of Technical and Further Education. Any place there for an economics specialist? She would have to check, later, she thought, but for the moment Ben's suggestion of a more leisurely lifestyle had a definite appeal, even if she would never admit that to him.

It was several days, in fact, before she got round to mentioning the subject to her father, whose reaction wasn't quite what Kate might have expected.

'Couple of months rest would do you the world of good,' he said first, almost parroting Ben's words. And Ben's overall arguments, Kate found as the discussion progressed.

She made no attempt, really, to try and change her father's mind. She was quite enjoying her life of relative leisure while realising it couldn't continue indefinitely. Sooner or later, she knew, a return to work would be needed just to keep her from becoming bored beyond belief.

'I'd be a lot happier if you'd wait a bit, Kate,' her father said, 'and I'm sure Ben doesn't want you to.' Whereupon she blew her top.

'What in God's green earth does Ben have to do with

this?' she cried, eyes wide with disbelief and sudden anger. 'My God! Does the man think he owns me, or what?'

'What are you so defensive about?' her father chided. 'He's concerned about you. What's wrong with that? Really, Kate, I think this hostility thing between you and Ben is quite ridiculous.'

'Well, there wouldn't be any hostility if he'd quit trying to run my life for me,' she snarled. 'Hasn't he got anything better to do?'

After the blow-up, however, she was ashamed enough to seek out her father and apologise, but the subject of her seeking a job was dropped by tactful, mutual consent.

In the meantime she slipped into a lazy, comfortable routine, doing the dawn fence patrol—sometimes with Robyn or Bill, but usually by herself—helping with the various outdoor tasks around the farm, and sometimes sharing the cooking chores to give Robyn a break.

Although Robyn continued to share the cottage with her brother, it seemed more logical and, indeed, comfortable, for all four of them to share their meals in the big house, where Robyn and Kate had found they were quite amenable to taking turnabout in the kitchen and sometimes combining their talents for special weekend treats.

It was a restful, almost idyllic existence, and Kate soon found herself relaxing in every aspect of her life. She worked with Bill in the yards, usually in the evenings when darkness helped to calm the skittish deer, and quickly became adept at administering the various drenches and worming medicines that were required.

She was fast friends with the two or three Judas deer, who helped, as did the donkeys, when it was time to shift the herds from paddock to paddock, or into the yards.

But it was the donkeys who remained her greatest friends, and she often extended her dawn patrol well into the morning as she invented, or at least became a willing participant in, various games to keep the intriguing animals amused.

All the red deer fawns had lost their pretty, spotted coats, assuming a dull brown-grey fur as autumn approached. The stags were almost in their finest condition, with enormous racks of antlers on the fallow bucks, and even the antlerless red deer gaining a majestic posture as they played and sparred in preparation for the coming mating season.

While Kate could understand the economics of having to velvet the stags, she sometimes thought it a pity. Compared to the single-antlered stag, the others looked . . . incomplete.

'They might not look as pretty, but they're a damned sight easier to handle,' her father commented when she spoke of it one evening. 'If we can figure out a way to do it properly next year, we'll velvet all the stags and the fallow bucks as well, although it will take some arranging, because the fallow deer are terribly spooky when it comes to being yarded. It's supposed to be easier at night, but I've got no great urge to get myself penned up with a mob of them without enough light to see what I'm about.'

The most common way of handling fallow deer, he told her, was through tranquillisation in the paddock. Some farmers, both in Australia and New Zealand, had tried various strategies for yarding the deer, but while some had miraculous success, others failed miserably using what appeared to be identical methods.

'That's where somebody like Bill is such an asset,' he said. And Kate couldn't but agree. Bill Campbell seemed almost a wild animal himself at times. He was incredibly calm, and moved among the deer without ever raising a whisker of fright, and his shyness among people wasn't far from that exhibited by the alert red deer hinds.

'Mind you, Ben's almost as good,' Henry Lyle continued, 'so we'll be glad of his help if there's anything that has to be done with the stags during the rut.'

Ah, Kate breathed. So Ben would be back—when? Late March or early April, she reasoned, when both red deer and fallow males would be at their peak of breeding excitement.

Or would it be even earlier than that? Bill had said something to her father about starting quite soon to separate the herds, leaving only sufficient stags with every breeding herd to maximise servicing without creating hostility and massive fights. The majority of stags and bucks would be penned on their own in paddocks as far removed as possible from the breeding herds.

But the days passed, and he didn't come, or even so much as telephone. And Kate found herself only thinking of him whenever somebody else brought out his name in conversation, or occasionally just as she was drifting into sleep at night.

She was so much more relaxed, now, and no longer the thin, harassed person she'd been on her arrival. She had put on just enough weight to change thin to slender, to take the harsher lines from her cheekbones, to soften the lines of her collarbones. And, she thought wryly, to force her into buying several new pairs of jeans, because she could hardly bend down in the old ones, and that not with any safety.

And she was tanned, too, despite the lateness of the season. Tanned all over, having found a tiny rock pool at the narrow end of the valley, far from the deer paddocks or from any evidence of human habitation. It was like being alone at the beginning of time, she thought, and tried to slip away for a swim and a sunbathing session every afternoon.

The pool was in a narrow creek running down into the farm proper, gushing forth from a tiny spring in bush so thick it was almost rain forest.

Kate had found it one day while on an extended hike, following a narrow, no-longer-used cattle pad that wove its way across the meadows and then into the timber. She supposed it was left over from when the property had originally been a dairy property, but after dozens of visits she considered it to be *her* creek, *her* track, and—most especially—*her* pool.

Not that she was selfish about it. She had asked Robyn along once or twice, only to find that Robyn preferred her swimming in the sea. 'Sharks, I can cope with, but the Australian bush has too many nasties to suit me,' she said, a reasonable enough comment considering the New Zealand bush contains no poisonous snakes, nor virtually anything else that might be considered dangerous.

Kate didn't worry about such things. She hadn't seen a single snake during any of her visits, and was frankly inclined in any event to believe that snakes wouldn't bother her if she didn't bother them. Besides, she thought, no snake would be impudent enough to try and bother her at *her* pool.

The hour-long walk required to reach the pool held a host of wonders for Kate, who had shed her city-bred habits and gained a rapport with rural living very quickly indeed. There was a resident echidna she encountered periodically, a family of kookaburras that greeted her visits with maniac screams and blatantly bludged scraps from her lunch. Hordes of tiny, brightly-coloured fish would throng around her in the water, sometimes nibbling at her toes and fingers.

But her favourite of all was the resident owner of the

next pool down but one, where a duck-billed platypus had its home. Her occasional sighting of this shy, usually nocturnal animal invariably gave her a thrill, knowing that most Australians would never see a live wild platypus in their entire lives.

At first she had thought the dark-furred beast was some kind of water-rat, but then it turned in the crystal clear water to give her a distinct view of its beaver's tail and duck-like bill. It had fled beneath an overhanging bank at her involuntary cry of delight, and thereafter she forced herself to silence when spying on the creature.

She no longer worried greatly about finding a job, either. Her father had been more than happy to turn over to her the book-keeping chores involved with the property, and it also fell to her to cope with the shopping and anything else that involved a trip to town.

That, she suspected, was a deliberate ploy by her father to avoid going to town himself, which he disliked, but also because he was subtly trying to encourage her to get out more, to meet people. She noticed he made no such attempt to broaden Robyn's social experience, and wondered at times about that, though she never mentioned it.

Certainly Robyn didn't seem to mind the isolation. She kept busy with housekeeping chores, cooking, and raising the small flocks of ducks, geese and chickens she was breeding up for the table.

Kate didn't mind the trips to town, though she rarely met anybody more interesting than grocery clerks despite her father's apparent hopes. She and Robyn took the occasional all-day trip to visit the beaches between Maroochydore and Noosa Heads, where both of them received complimentary glances from late-season holidaymakers, but by tacit, unspoken agreement, no fraternisation was encouraged.

Also by unspoken agreement, nothing was ever said by either of them about Robyn's relationship with Kate's father. The two women got on so well that Kate felt sure Robyn needed no reassurance about Kate's feelings on the matter, and indeed she had come to rather hope that something would develop.

Under the watchful eyes of the two women, Henry Lyle had regained his health and colour, and looked much more his old self. He slept, as Kate did, ten and sometimes twelve hours a night, and no longer showed any signs of overwork. He looked and seemed both healthy and happy, to everyone's pleasure.

But if there was anything between him and Robyn except genuine friendship, it was kept well hidden from Kate. He was always courteous, complimentary about Robyn's cooking, and invariably ready to laugh with her. He often chose to help Robyn with the dishes, and indeed they spent a great deal of time together, but with no sign of any romantic development, which occasionally left Kate feeling vaguely disappointed.

Never a harsh word, she thought. Never a disagreement. It's not romance. And no wonder—it's boredom!

It was that horrid, sobering thought which drove Kate to break her vow of non-involvement, at least to the point of attempting what she thought was a subtle approach to Robyn on the subject.

The response was a tinkle of amused laughter, followed by a lecture of gentle but determined severity.

'Kate, you're about as subtle as Ben,' Robyn chuckled. 'And about as impatient, although you, at least, have your youth as an excuse. Your father and I are getting along just fine, thank you. I know it doesn't all look very exciting, at least from your point of view, but think about it from ours. Your father had nearly thirty years with a woman he loved very dearly, and still loves. A man like him doesn't just turn that on and off like a water tap.

'And I, my dear, am by nature a very, very cautious creature. I may talk more than my brother, and be much more outgoing, but we're very much alike inside. I'm too damned cautious, to be honest, which is why I'm still a spinster at my age despite being a fair looking specimen.'

'Better than fair,' Kate interjected, 'and really, Robyn, I don't mean to pry, but . . .'

'But of course you meant to pry,' the older woman replied with a fond grin. 'And I'm honoured that you care enough about both of us to be concerned. So do us all a favour, Kate. Stay concerned, but just exactly as you have been. At our age, Henry and I can manage our lives *without* any matchmaking.'

'Point taken, and I'm sorry I brought it up,' Kate replied. 'It's just that you both seemed so . . .'

'Bored?' Robyn grinned hugely. 'Try comfortable, dear. Much more accurate. Although compared to your rather tempestuous affair with Ben, I suppose it does all seem a bit boring. Speaking of which—now that you've given me a legitimate excuse to ask—how are things between you and Ben, anyway?'

'Touchée,' replied Kate. 'Now I really wish I'd kept my mouth shut! Although actually I can say with total honesty that there's nothing at all between Ben Croft and me. I haven't so much as spoken to him since I put him on the plane last month with what you call his little Chinese fortune cookie.'

'My little joke, dear. She's much more tart than cookie, I suspect,' Robyn replied drily. 'But where did she come into all this? Was she lying in wait for him at the airport? It wouldn't surprise me.'

'Not exactly,' Kate replied with a grin of her own. 'But she was apparently expecting to find him here.' She went on to relate the details of the incident, even to the goodbye kiss and the Oriental response to it.

'Magnificent!' Robin exclaimed when they'd both had a good laugh about it. 'Oh, and I'm glad you told me. I just love having something to torment dear Ben with.'

'Oh, you wouldn't!' Kate squealed, more for her own sake than Ben's.

'Just watch me,' Robyn retorted. 'Watch very carefully; you just might learn something.'

'Oh, but you can't,' Kate pleaded, only to be laughed at in the gentlest possible manner.

'What possible difference could it make?' Robyn chided, 'since you insist there's nothing between you in the first place. Or would you like to change that story now? Has a little time apart made you have a decent look at Ben?'

'Not a bit,' Kate replied stubbornly. 'I merely don't want to be embarrassed by anything you might decide to say to him. He means nothing to me whatsoever.'

'Oh, Kate, stop fooling yourself,' Robyn sighed. 'One mention of Ben Croft's name and you start slinking back into that grieving widow role, which doesn't suit you at all, despite a pretty fair acting job. Your husband's been dead a fair while now, and unless I'm sadly mistaken you don't miss him one little bit!'

The vestiges of Kate's guilt flared into new life, and she turned her eyes away, seeking to end the conversation, but Robyn wouldn't let her.

Ignoring Kate's muttered, 'That's not true,' she drove in forcefully, revealing an astonishing comprehension of the entire sordid marraige. Finally, unable to stand up against such astute observation, Kate broke down and confessed her guilt, both about Wayne's death and her own ineffectual failure as a marriage partner. But if she expected sympathy, she was mightily mistaken.

'What utter rubbish!' Robyn sneered. 'Rubbish! Do you hear me, Kate Lyle? My God, what a sorry little tale!'

Kate, mouth open in surprise at the vehemence of the assault, backed away, only to find Robyn staunchly following her.

'So you made a mistake. So you got hooked up with a proper bastard. And you couldn't cope with it because you were young and naïve and not too awfully swift either. So you wished the swine dead and he died. So *what*! My God, child, what would you expect? Do you think you're some kind of saint?

'It's obvious the devil made your life hell while he was alive—do you want to let him ruin it for you from the grave as well?'

Robyn paused for breath, but not long enough for Kate to interject. 'And I suppose it's this ridiculous guilt complex that's had you keeping Ben at arm's length, too? Or is it just that you can't think of yourself as being woman enough to handle a proper man? Well, maybe you can't, but you'll sure as hell not find out if you don't at least try.'

'No!' Kate cried, 'No. That's not it! I . . . I know the guilt thing is something I must learn to cope with, but it's more than that. It's that—oh, with Wayne I was a meek, submissive little doormat. It isn't surprising he walked all over me. But I'm not like that any more. I'm not! If anything I'm too much the opposite; I'm not going to let any man dominate me ever again . . .' She broke off, suddenly lost for words.

'And you can't see a relationship with a strong, dominant man like Ben Croft without you being submissive?' Robyn replied gently. 'Oh, Kate, you poor confused child!'

And to Kate's surprise she folded her into her arms with a gesture that could only be considered motherly. It was all that was needed; the dam wall surrounding her guilt and her fragile ego fell into shreds, releasing a torrent of tears that left her, some minutes later, trembling with relief.

Robyn left her, then, long enough to make them a pot of tea and ensure that her father and Bill weren't on their way back to the house. And once the tea was ready, she gave Kate a solid helping of womanly advice.

'It isn't the solid, strong men like Ben you have to worry about,' she began. 'Oh, he'll dominate you if you let him, of course, but he's no child; he doesn't have to prove anything. Don't forget that if he really wanted a submissive woman, Kim Lee would have snared him long ago. In fact,' she sighed, 'I think the way you've been dealing with him—except for your real reasons—has been just about right. Well, maybe a bit *too* abrasive. But at least he's interested. You can't deny that.'

'Don't be so sure,' Kate replied. 'And it doesn't really matter that much, because I'm not really sure about my own feelings in any event. But I'd guess I've turned him right off.'

'Well, we'll soon find out,' Robyn retorted with a glance out the window. 'Because unless I'm sadly mistaken, he's just coming now.'

CHAPTER SIX

WHATEVER else Robyn might have planned to say was lost.

'Oh, *no!*' Kate wailed, and immediately fled, thundering up the stairs to her room. Bad enough that Ben had chosen to arrive unannounced, but for him to find her with swollen red eyes from weeping would open the door to far too many questions.

Kate spent nearly ten minutes dabbing at her eyes with cold water and tidying her hair, but she refrained from any make-up at all, and decided not to bother changing her clothes either. Ben had seen her before in jeans and a shirt, she reasoned, and would, in fact, expect her to be wearing such gear.

But when she returned downstairs, it was to find her hurried exit had been in vain. Ben hadn't even stopped at the house, Robyn informed her wryly, but had driven straight on to the yards with no more than a general wave as he'd passed.

It was nearly half an hour later when his vehicle returned, half an hour in which Robyn forced Kate to help her with new plans for dinner that evening in a vain attempt to keep Kate's mind off the impending confrontation.

'Don't be so edgy,' she said accusingly. 'He's just a man, like any other man, and since he's probably spent most of the past month pandering to little Miss Kung Fu, he probably won't be fit for normal feminine company anyway.'

'Thank you, Robyn. That does *so* much for my confidence,' Kate replied with a sarcastic sneer. 'Just exactly what I needed.'

'Might as well be realistic as the way you are,' Robyn shrugged. 'Besides, why should you care? *You* don't even like the man, or have you forgotten that?'

'Please, Robyn . . . if you want to torment somebody, save it for later. I've had about all I can take for one day,' Kate pleaded.

'Oh, hooey. You're young and healthy; you can take it,' was the bland reply. 'Might as well get you warmed up for later, because while you might have changed over the past month, I can't imagine Ben doing the same. He'll be his normal, beautiful, lovable, arrogant self.'

'You forgot charming,' Kate laughed, only to be told sarcastically that, 'He's always that.'

And he was, although with a month of relaxation behind her Kate found Ben's attitude suspiciously easy-going.

He sauntered in the door, elegant in very expensive slacks, open-necked shirt and shoes once shiny but now dusty from the yards, and with a broad smile on his face.

'By God, but you're lovely. Both of you!' he grinned, stooping to plant a perfunctory kiss on each of them in turn. 'I really don't know why I stayed away so long, with all this pulchritude stashed away out here in the bush.'

'I can't imagine,' Robyn replied drily. Kate said nothing at all, having enough trouble merely meeting his open appraisal.

'Don't be sarcastic, Robyn. It doesn't become you,' he replied lightly, never taking his eyes from Kate's. 'If you can't say anything nice, don't say anything at all. Like Kate here,' he added with a wry grin.

'What's the matter, Kate? Don't tell me you've been stunned into silence by my handsome, charming personage and rapier wit?'

'Actually,' she replied after a moment's silence in which she carefully chose her words, 'it's your modesty that's overwhelmed me.'

'Hah! Well done,' he grinned. 'For a minute there I thought you might be sick or something, and we couldn't have that.'

'Oh, just keep it up and I'm sure you'll manage,' she retorted, warming to the repartee and mildly surprised to find how much she was actually enjoying it.

'Sorry, not right now. Too much to do,' he replied. 'I'm off to get changed and I'll be in the yards with Bill if anybody wants me. Not that I expect anybody will.'

And with a casual wave and a 'See you at dinner,' he was gone as flamboyantly as he'd arrived. Kate and Robyn stood looking at each other, wondering at this lighthearted, casual image, but neither said anything until a denim-clad Ben had left the house a minute later en route to the yards.

'Well!' said Robyn. 'That was interesting. I think. Better watch it, Kate, he's up to something.'

'No kidding?' Kate replied with a shake of her head.

'Too right! That, my dear, is the Ben Croft I remember from his early days in New Zealand, when he was wheeling-and-dealing his way to the top. He's got something up his sleeve besides an arm, and whatever it is, he's all set to enjoy it. You could just see the adrenalin flowing.'

'Ye-es,' Kate mused thoughtfully, not quite ready to admit that she'd been admiring something besides adrenalin in her appraisal of the tall, muscular figure. It was no consolation that Ben certainly did have something up his sleeve, and she had the unholy fear that it somehow involved herself.

Forewarned is forearmed, she tried to tell herself as she carefully dressed for dinner that evening. She chose a simple, flowing caftan in various shades of green in a striped pattern, and judiciously applied her make-up to match. The caftan, while simple in line, flowed elegantly but covered her from throat to toes.

Although just what being covered so thoroughly was supposed to accomplish, she didn't really know, but it did give her a sense of well-being, almost of protection.

Ben arrived in the lounge room wearing, of all things, a tie. Which caused Robyn to mutter 'Oh-oh!' beneath her breath at Kate, who was standing beside her. The rest of his attire, a Harris tweed sports jacket and casual slacks, was quite in keeping, but the tie was a definite caution flag. While the men of Kathryn Downs made a policy of dressing for dinner, it was the casual, comfortable 'dress' of subtropical Queensland, where ties were considered right only for weddings, funerals and politicians.

Even Henry Lyle raised a faintly quizzical eyebrow at the sight of the tie, something he had personally sworn never to wear again after leaving the advertising business to take up deer farming. Bill Campbell, who had never worn a tie in his life, didn't give it a second glance.

'You're looking very spiffy tonight, Mr Croft,' said Robyn, determined as usual to open the fireworks. 'Have you come to sell us all life insurance or something?'

Kate winced, fervently wishing that Robyn wouldn't so blatantly seek to score off Ben. She could only lose, and she must surely know it.

But this night, it seemed, she would be boxing with shadows. Ben looked down at his clothing and then at Robyn with a blank expression. 'What's the matter with this?' he asked blandly. 'Am I too pretty for you or something? It's hardly as fancy as what you're wearing,' with a connoisseur's appraisal of Robyn's expensive dress, 'or Kate.' And this time the glance was frankly, sensually appraising. 'What are you two selling?'

'Only superb food, from my point of view,' Robyn replied. 'Kate can speak for herself.'

Oh, damn you, Robyn! Kate fumed inwardly. If you want to play up to him, fine, but leave me out of it.

'Coffee at two bob the cup,' she quipped, taking up Robyn's lead with little enthusiasm.

'That cheap?' His eyes were lit with unholy fires. 'I wouldn't have expected you to put such a low price on your . . . talents, Kate.'

'It doesn't take a great deal of talent to make a good cup of coffee,' she replied sweetly. 'Would you like a drink?'

'Yes, please. Whisky and water,' he replied, 'but don't bother moving; I'll get it myself.' And he did, which at least allowed Kate a slight breather.

Damn him! Is he going to play word games all night? she wondered. She could already feel tension building in her tummy, and despite an earlier promise not to let him get to her, she knew it wouldn't be easy.

'And what have you been doing with yourself while I've been gone?' he asked a moment later, drink in hand. 'I must say you look . . . rested. And you've put on weight, which is nice.'

'Depending on your viewpoint,' she muttered, then, more loudly, 'Not a great deal, really. Just helping out where I can.'

'Don't be modest, Kate,' her father interjected. 'Taking over the books for this operation may not be much to you, but it's a millstone from around my neck.'

'Ah,' Ben replied with a sharkish smile and too, too much feigned interest, 'I gather, then, that you haven't found that job we were talking about?'

As you very well know, Kate thought, though she replied with a simple, 'No.'

'Not even looking?' The light in his eyes had changed,

she saw with alarm. Now he looked tigerish, ready to pounce.

What are you leading up to? she wondered, thinking quickly, then chose a disarming—she hoped—reply.

'No, I thought I'd take your advice and have a good rest first,' she said sweetly, trembling inside at having to admit such a thing and quite afraid it was just the reply he'd been hoping for.

'Good,' he said without a change of expression. 'And if I may say so, it appears to have done you the world of good.'

Kate didn't reply, waiting for him to continue. Surely now he'd make some snooty comment about how she should obviously take advice from him more often, or some such thing.

But no! Instead, surprisingly, he merely nodded as if very pleased with himself and turned to speak to her father about business affairs, leaving Kate with all her defences up and the enemy no longer in sight.

She turned away herself, wondering about it all, only to meet a comparably quizzical expression in Robyn's glance. Robyn merely shrugged, but Kate remained frankly apprehensive even when they had finished their drinks and streamed in to dinner.

During the meal, which Robyn and Kate served up in turns, Ben was glibly charming, carrying the conversation with a smooth geniality and dispersing compliments right and left.

'If it wasn't that Henry and Bill would lynch me, I'd set you two up in a restaurant,' he quipped. 'Or have you had enough of the restaurant trade for ever, Robyn?'

'Not necessarily,' Robyn replied, to Kate's astonishment. 'Although it would certainly depend on the offer.'

'And how about you, Kate?' His question was lightly

put, but he had that look in his eye again, and Kate
answered cautiously.

'I've never tried it, so I don't really know,' she said. 'It
might be fun, with Robyn.'

'Well then, forget it!' The comment, surprisingly,
growled from her father's mouth. 'If you go, you go on
your own.'

'Why, Henry, I didn't know you cared!' From Robyn,
this comment, accompanied by a wild fluttering of eyelas-
hes and maidenly simpering.

'Hummph! Time you did, then,' Henry Lyle retorted
grumpily, as if surprised himself by the vehemence of his
earlier remark.

Everyone but he, it seemed, flashed glances of surprise
and pleasure round the table, but it was Ben who spoke up
next. And, rather to Kate's surprise, he didn't pick up on
the obvious, but blithely changed the subject entirely,
embarking on a nearly-ribald story about Vietnam, or was
it Hong Kong? Kate wasn't really listening, her ears and
heart full at the unexpected revelation that her father really
was interested in Robyn.

How splendid, she thought, and how splendid of Ben to
hurry them past what might, perhaps, have been a difficult
moment. Very diplomatic.

Without really thinking, she flashed him a brilliant
smile, a wide, honest expression of her happiness and well-
being. And, she realised later, of her gratitude.

They lingered less than usual over coffee and liqueurs,
and when Bill excused himself with a slow, pleased smile
at his sister, it was left to Ben to take the hint because Kate
didn't catch the significance until he spoke.

'Come, Kate. We'll leave the dishes and I'll help you
with them later,' he said, rising lithely to his feet and
taking her by the arm. Before she could think to protest, he

had escorted her out on to the porch, grabbing up her shawl from the coat rack as they passed.

Once outside, however, common sense returned and Kate snatched her arm way. 'Do you mind?' she hissed. 'And what was all that about?'

'My God, but you're dense, sometimes,' he hissed back. 'Or did I misinterpret that glowing smile you bestowed upon me earlier? Even with your astounding naïvety you should understand a little thing like giving privacy to people at high emotional moments.'

'Oh,' she replied dimly.

'Exactly. And since you've finally trundled your father out of his complacency, it's only proper now to let him re-establish his own terms of reference. Right?'

'Oh!' she said again, but with a greatly different inflection this time. 'You *smug* bastard!'

His teeth flashed in the moonlight. 'Hardly smug, dear Kate, but certainly pleased—as I'm sure you are—that they've finally started to get their act together.'

'No,' she said, 'smug! You deliberately set that up. My God, but you must get a lot of sadistic pleasure out of organising other people's lives for them!'

'What the hell are you on about?' he growled. 'I did no such thing. I was merely throwing out compliments about a most excellent meal. I didn't know it was going to lead to that!'

'I'll just bet you didn't,' snapped Kate, tongue dripping venom. Then she spun away from him and walked swiftly away towards the yards, tripping delicately in her high heels, but making fair enough headway.

It was no surprise to find Ben instantly beside her, but he made no attempt to touch her, until she struck a rut and would have fallen but for his quick grasp on her arm. Once she was steady again, however, he immediately released her before she could snap at him.

Through the yards and into the long run between the deer paddocks they walked, Ben slowing his stride to match Kate's less easy one. And once they had reached the first of the stag paddocks, Kate stopped. It was silly to have walked this far, she thought. It wasn't, obviously, going to free her from Ben's attention, and she had only the long, stumbling trek back to look forward to.

Leaning against one of the tall strainer posts, she looked up to where a high strong wind was scudding wisps of cloud about across the path of the almost full moon.

'Beautiful, isn't it?' He seemed to be reading her thoughts, but the tranquillity of the scene kept the bitterness from her reply.

'Yes, it is,' she said. 'Unbelievably so.'

'Ought to be Henry and Robyn out here, by rights. They're probably just in the mood for a full moon and all.' He chuckled. 'Instead, I'll bet they're busy doing up the dishes, despite my having volunteered us to do it.'

Kate had to laugh. 'You're joking,' she said.

'Want to bet?' He took her silence for confirmation. 'Okay . . . if the dishes are still waiting when we get back, I'll do them myself,' he said.

'Umm . . . and if they're not?' she asked suspiciously.

'You get to help.'

It took a moment to sink in; then she burst into peals of laughter. 'That's ridiculous!'

'Uh-huh. So's life, sometimes. Like us being out here snarling at each other when there are far better things to do,' he said softly, and even as she realised he was whispering right in her ear, she felt his lips caress her neck.

'Don't!' She didn't flinch away, but at the word his lips were gone leaving only the delicious touch of their passage. She shivered.

'You're cold. Do you want to go back?'

'I'm not cold at all,' she denied, ignoring the second question. She didn't want to go back at all, but she wasn't going to tell him so directly.

What she really wanted, in fact, was for him to kiss her again—properly. But she wasn't going to tell him that, either.

Kate heard the click of his lighter, and smelled the pungent odour of tobacco just before he reached out to pass the already-lit cigarette to her without being asked. Another click, obviously for his own.

So he wasn't going to kiss her again, she thought rather sadly. And then—damn you, Kate, you don't know what you want! But then why was she so strongly conscious of the nearness of him, of the faint, masculine scent of his after-shave drifting in the night air?

They stood there, neither saying a word, until the cigarettes were finished and carefully stubbed out beneath Ben's shoe. Kate glanced into the paddock, her eyes caught by a slight movement and then widening in terror as she recognised the fast-paced advance of the farm's sole antlered red stag.

His mighty rack gleamed in the bright moonlight, and his eyes were like those of a devil as he pranced towards them, flinging his great head around and snorting loudly. Kate stood spellbound until something grabbed her by the arm and flung her away just as the stag struck the fence just exactly where she had been leaning.

He staggered from the impact, then shook his head until he had cleared the huge antlers from their impalement of the wire, and stepped back several paces into the paddock.

Head flung back until the antlers lay across his shoulders like the branches of a huge tree, he stretched open his mouth and bellowed—an unearthly, banshee sound that poured into the night, the bawl of an angry bull mixed with the roar of a lion and the scream of a soul in torment.

Kate turned away from the sheer volume of the sound, unashamedly writhing closer into the strong arms that wrapped protectively around her, her face buried against the softness of Ben's shirt, revelling in the warmth of him, the strength of him.

Again the stag roared, screaming his devilish defiance, his challenge to other, lesser stags who might dare to oppose him.

'Look!' Kate turned at Ben's urgent whisper, twisting so as to stay within the cage of his arms, but looking where he did. Her eyes widened with excitement as she saw another stag, this one antlerless and considerably smaller than the first, circling in towards them from one side. Across the paddock, a mob of hinds had also gathered, responding to the defiant bellow of their lord and master, but looking for all the world like harpies gathered to watch a hanging.

The young stag bellowed, his challenging bugle a puny reply to that of the master. He pranced forward, flinging his head as if he, too, had the vicious rack of antlers with which to fight.

'He'll be killed,' Kate whispered, wanting to look away but unable to do it. She was riveted to the scene.

'No chance,' Ben whispered. 'He's not tough enough to tackle the old stag and he knows it. He's just keeping the old fellow on his toes, though he wouldn't be averse to stealing a hind or two if he gets the chance.'

True. Even as they watched, the youngster circled away from any risk of true conflict, and a moment later the entire herd had drifted to the far side of the paddock, leaving only Ben and Kate near the fence.

From a far paddock, another stag bayed his challenge, his voice echoing in the distance to be answered by still another. Then, for a long moment, there was silence. Kate moved to free herself, not really wanting to, yet knowing she must, but Ben turned her in his arms and dropped his mouth easily to meet her lips.

There was nothing demanding in his kiss; it held none of the violence, the sheer sexuality they had just witnessed. His lips moved across hers with gentle, persuasive pressure, seeking response, requesting it, but not demanding.

Kate's own lips softened, shifting to meet his caress with a gentle pressure of their own, but she didn't move otherwise, and Ben only held her sufficiently to keep her close to him. And after some time he ended it, gently, but firmly and deliberately, shifting his arms to designate her freedom.

'See,' he whispered, 'we could get to be friends yet.' And he said it so gently, so seriously, that she couldn't even take offence.

They turned away then, strolling hand-in-hand back through the now-silent deer yards towards the house without speaking. Kate didn't need words; she was becoming all too certain of her feelings, but unfortunately she was no more sure than ever about how Ben really felt. And, she feared, it would be some time—if ever—before she did know.

But it was a great incentive, very great indeed, when they paused at the foot of the stairs and he kissed her again, saying, 'I meant what I said earlier, Kate. The rest has done marvels for you; you look wonderful.'

If I look so 'wonderful', why this sudden change in tactics? she asked herself once she was alone in her room. Not that she really wanted a repeat of his earlier, more rugged approach, and yet . . . his kisses tonight had seemed very *friendly*. She wasn't sure she really liked that, but on the other hand she had certainly enjoyed them.

Morning came with a rush of activity. Kate woke early, having spent a more restless night than usual. And her first thought was for the left-over dishes and Ben's ridiculous bet. Slipping into her jeans and shirt, she ran a comb quickly through her hair, wrapped it in a loose chignon, and trotted downstairs and into the kitchen.

'Morning. I wondered if you'd remember,' came a caustic voice from one corner of the table. 'And you promised to help, too.'

'Well, obviously I did,' she quipped. 'The dishes are done, aren't they?'

'Coffee's ready, too. Want some?'

'Yes, but I'll get it,' she replied with a grin, and surreptitiously brushed her hand along the edge of the sink as she passed on her way to the percolator. Cool! Perhaps too cool, she thought suspiciously. But she kept quiet about it until she had poured her own coffee, topped up his and sat down across from him.

'Well?'

'Well what?' He wasn't smiling, but his eyes were alight with subdued laughter.

'You know very well. Did you win your bet or didn't you?'

'Well, you should know; you just claimed to have helped.'

'Which means you're not going to tell me, I suppose,' she mused. 'Doesn't matter, I'll find out eventually.'

He didn't answer immediately, and then whatever he was going to say was lost in the arrival of Robyn and Bill, followed a moment later by Henry Lyle.

'Kate's going to ask who did the dishes from last night, and you're not to tell her or you're all fired!' Ben cried before anyone could so much as say good morning.

Her father looked at Robyn; Robyn looked at Kate; they all looked at Ben, and then Robyn blurted out, 'Okay, I'll play. Who did do the dishes?'

'It was the good fairy, obviously,' Henry answered.

Bill, as usual, said nothing.

Then there was a long silence as Kate stared at each in turn, trying through sheer will power to force out an answer. 'You're all impossible!' she wailed, unsure whether she wanted to laugh or cry.

'Better than being fired, especially this early in the morning,' her father growled as he thrust himself into his chair. 'I don't even care who made the coffee; all I want to know is who's pouring it for me.'

'I hope you're fitter than you sound, Henry,' said Ben. 'We're going to be busy today. In case any of you missed the commotion last night, the rut appears to have started, at least among the reds. And judging from some reports I've heard from Victoria, I think we'd better start shifting every animal we have that's anywhere near the front boundary fence.'

'Poachers?' Bill, who hadn't seemed even to be listening, voiced the problem in a single word.

'I hope not,' Ben replied. 'We've had no problems, but more and more people are getting to know about us, and there's been a spate of publicity recently from New South Wales and Victoria, where they're having no end of troubles. It could come here as well.'

'Better to shift the fallows at night.' It wasn't a full sentence, but it was more words in one string than Kate had ever heard Bill utter.

'We'll do all the actual shifting at night, I think,' Ben replied, 'but we'll have to spend today planning the operation and checking which paddocks have the best feed and everything.'

'Do you really think there's a likelihood of trouble?' Henry asked. 'We're pretty isolated back here; I shouldn't think we'd attract all that much notice.'

'Let's just hope you're right,' Ben replied gravely. 'But on the other hand don't forget the problems they encountered in Victoria when deer farming was legalised. The hunter groups objected mightily to the legalisation, and while I'm not totally convinced it was legitimate hunters who were involved in these latest hassles, I do think it's the kind of thing that could spread all too easily.'

'I don't understand,' said Kate. 'Why should hunters want to oppose deer farming in the first place?'

'It's a long story,' Ben replied. 'But what it boils down to is that some deer farm stock has come from the wild, and some hunters reckon the deer farmers are capturing deer that should really be left as a breeding pool for wild deer. They've got a point, too, since deer hunting in Australia hasn't been developed nearly as much as it might have been, looking purely at the recreational viewpoint.

'But,' he continued, 'what they seem to forget is that the build-up of deer farms has vastly increased interest in deer at the government level, and I think—hope—that eventually we'll see that interest extend to producing some long-term programmes aimed at improving the hunting situation. We could even find, eventually, deer farms providing seed stock for wild populations, much as trout hatcheries now do in some areas.'

Robyn came into the conversation at that point. 'The problems here are nothing like what's happening in New Zealand,' she said. 'There, protection of farmed deer is a really major aspect of deer farming, because of course deer are counted as a pest in the wild, have been shot by everybody for years and years, and still provide a major economic factor as a game animal. In fact some German markets won't accept venison as proper game unless it's from deer that have been killed in the wild. Farmed deer simply aren't considered game.'

'But what about right here?' Kate asked. 'Surely there's nobody in this district who's likely to be specifically looking at shooting our deer.'

'Don't bet on it,' Ben replied. 'There's a hooligan element everywhere, and that's exactly what I'm concerned with here. Especially for the antlered bucks and stags, who'd provide a bit too tempting a target for any young punk who has a gun and wants to kill something. Or just shoot something, for that matter. You've only to drive the country roads and look at the number of shot-up road signs to realise that. That's why we're going to shift as many deer as possible as far from the road as possible, just to remove temptation, as it were.'

He paused, looking thoughtful for a moment. 'And also,' he said then, 'I think it might be better if you didn't make your morning patrols alone, Kate.'

'Oh, really! Don't you think that's going a bit far?'

'No, frankly, I don't. But just so you don't think I'm picking on you, we'll put it to the vote,' he said.

And when the three men left to begin their work, Kate turned on Robyn viciously. 'Thanks a lot!' she sneered. 'That was a great blow you struck for feminism, voting with the men as you did.'

'You be a feminist if you like,' Robyn replied calmly. 'All I'll say is that I was voting *for* Ben, not *against* you. And the reason is simply that I agree with him. Frankly, I think you should be flattered that he was concerned.'

'Concern is one thing and chauvinism is another,' Kate replied.

'And pigheadedness is something else again. Now stop being silly and come and help me with the dishes, unless that's against your feminine principles too,' said Robyn. 'Don't let your feelings for Ben colour every single aspect of your relationship. It's unhealthy.'

'Humph!' Kate snorted. 'I still think it's chauvinistic.' But she helped with the dishes nonetheless, taking out her bad temper on a stubbornly-stained frying pan.

When the men returned to sit discussing their herd movement ideas over lunch, Kate remained silent, using her eyes and attitude to tell Ben Croft she still considered him to be wrong. He ignored her, which did nothing to improve her mood.

That evening, however, she forgot about the issues of the morning in her excitement with the work at hand.

They were all involved, and before the final herd move had been accomplished, Kate was ready to admit that half a dozen more people would have been welcome. Not that the work was overly hard; it was just that the deer seemed to be picking up the human nervousness—mostly her own, she thought—and insisted on showing uncommon stubbornness about being shifted to where Ben wanted them.

At one point, where Kate was on the end of a three-person fence in which she, Ben and Bill carried a long length of building plastic as a sort of movable deer-driver, she had the distinct feeling the deer were simply laughing at them. Each time they had the small herd of fallow deer close to the gate through which they were supposed to go, the doe which led the herd would decide she didn't like the gate.

From a tranquil, slow-walking, peaceful mob, the deer would suddenly leap into frenetic action, leaping back past and sometimes even over the plastic barrier to regain the far end of the paddock. There, they transformed instantly again to being placid, grazing as if nothing had occurred to disturb them.

'It's maddening,' she muttered when the team stopped for a quiet smoke and a re-think of the situation. 'Why are they acting up like this?'

'Sheer contrariness,' Ben grinned. He didn't seem at all concerned by their failure. 'We'll leave them for now and see about that stag herd we put the donkeys in with. With no fickle female among them, they may be easier to handle.'

Which, to Kate's chagrin, they were. And it was even more annoying to find that the fallow herd, when being shifted by the three men, also seemed to settle remarkably and were quickly relocated.

'It must be my perfume,' Kate complained lightly as they all headed back to the house. She was feeling quite put out, not really because of Ben's chauvinistic remarks, but because she felt she had been less than totally helpful in the work.

'Oh, I don't know,' Ben replied from beside her. 'I think your perfume's rather nice, myself. But then I'm not a deer.'

'I've always thought you were,' Robyn chimed in, and even Ben had the decency to groan. Kate didn't think it at all humorous.

Her moodiness kept her from sleeping well, although by morning she had come to terms with the fact that it was her own temperament as much as anything that was at fault. She dressed and slipped down to the kitchen, determined to try and get through this day, at least, without allowing Ben to get on her nerves.

She just had the coffee ready when the kitchen door opened and Ben slipped inside, padding along silently in stockinged feet.

'You look bright and sparkling this morning,' he said cheerily. 'Looking forward to sharing your morning stroll?'

Twit! Of course I'm not looking forward to it, she thought, and said, 'I suppose it might make a nice change.'

'Good,' he said, then lapsed into thoughtful silence as he sipped at the coffee she poured him. Kate, too, slipped into a reverie, emerging only when he repeated a question.

'I asked what you were thinking,' he said. 'You were frowning, so it can't have been very nice.'

'Oh, it was nothing important,' she replied, keeping her eyes on her coffee.

'Which means you think it's none of my business,' he prodded, 'or are you usually so quiet and withdrawn in the morning?'

'It's the best time of the day,' she replied. 'But not for . . . talking. I just sort of like to come fully awake gradually, without having to think too much.'

'Hmm. I was just thinking how like the stereotyped married couple we are, sitting here in glum silence because we've either nothing to say or we've said it all before.'

It was so close to what Kate had really been thinking that she started nervously. He didn't seem to notice.

'But of course it's not like that at all,' he continued. 'Tell me, Kate, were you like this with your husband in the mornings, or did you talk to each other over your coffee?'

She stiffened, instinctively fearing his prying tone. How could she reply? Be honest, admitting she'd hardly ever seemed to talk with Wayne? Much less early in the mornings, when he was usually at his grumpiest. She had listened, in the mornings. In fact, thinking back, it seemed she had always listened. Wayne had never considered that she might have an opinion he would bother to listen to.

It was at that instant Kate realised she hadn't thought

about Wayne, or her disastrous marriage, for days ...
weeks, perhaps. And I wouldn't have now, she raged
inwardly, if you hadn't brought it up.

'No,' she said then, and didn't bother to expand on it.
Let Ben put whatever inflection on it he wanted to.

'All right,' he replied. 'Then I won't bother you with
conversation during our walk. Are you ready to leave
now?'

And that was it. Without another single word he slipped
into his boots, held the door for her, and walked beside
her, indeed usually a step or two behind her, as they
patiently inspected the fences and the condition of the
herds. Only when the ever-vigilant donkeys spotted them
and rushed up for their handouts of apple did he speak.
And then it was to the animals, as if Kate hadn't even
been there.

Doing, she thought, exactly what he thought she wanted.
And it was insufferably annoying. Because she could sense
him wanting to talk to her, to point out the small mob of
wallabies just outside the fence with words, rather than a
mute gesture, to explain why he would stop to specifically
look at one particular deer, one specific section of fencing.

By the time they got back to the house she realised that
her own attitude, her own words, had prevented their
walk from being something shared; she had forced Ben
into making it a stroll in which two strangers shared
nothing but the same direction. Worse, she realised she
had missed something, some real opportunity to at least
try and understand this complex man.

He remained strangely silent during breakfast, though
Robyn's normal chatter more than made up for the lack.
And immediately the meal was finished, Ben retreated to
the office, giving Kate no opportunity to apologise for her
rudeness.

There was less opportunity at lunch, with everyone else at table with them, and the meal was no sooner over than Ben announced to no one in particular that he was going into town and might not be back for dinner. No explanation, of course, nothing that might have given Kate any room to suggest she would like to go along. And worse, nothing to suggest he might have liked to have her along.

'Not that he should have,' she muttered to herself as she sprawled on *her* rock, in *her* swimming hole, feeling strangely lonely for the very first time in a place that had always given her comfort.

Damn the man anyway. She didn't need a new man in her life, didn't want one, and in any event she seemed only to be at odds with Ben all the time. But even then she was drawn to him, and she was beginning to feel less and less sure that it was purely a physical reaction.

Dabbling one toe in the cool, crystal water, she idly speculated what her reaction might be were he to suddenly step from the bush and find her sunbathing naked as she was.

No speculation about his reaction; she could guess that easily enough, she thought. If she ordered him away, he would leave instantly. But if she didn't . . .?

'Good afternoon, sir. Enjoying your stroll?' she said. No . . . a bit too formal. Indeed, much too formal.

'Care to join me, sir? The sun's warm and the water's cool.' That sounded just a bit twee, she thought.

So how about, 'Come on in; the water's fine'? Well, maybe. A bit hackneyed, though.

As the mid-afternoon sun lulled her to drowsiness, Kate hedged around the opening conversational gambit and let her senses fantasise instead on what might happen . . . later.

In the euphoric state of her daydream she could once

again taste Ben's lips on hers, feel the touch of his hands on her body, feel her body reacting, taking control of mind and conscience . . . and heart.

'My God!' she cried aloud. 'I'm already more than half in love with the man.'

A sobering, yet tantalising thought, and one that seemed somehow to sharpen the edges of the sunlight, delineate the shadows and bring her senses to new life. The small glade around her pool took on a fantasy texture, became a garden.

She lay back, eyes closed, visualising herself and Ben, complete with traditional fig-leaves. Then she opened her eyes, and saw the snake—and squealed in alarm.

It wasn't a large snake, and it wasn't doing anything but swim across one corner of the pool. Nowhere near Kate, and certainly no threat except to her peace of mind.

It was gone, indeed, before the echoes of her frightened cry had died, wriggling silently into the tall grass across the pool from her.

But it was a snake . . . a snake in *her* garden. And Kate couldn't but wonder if it mightn't be prophetic, somehow. Her mood broken, shattered with her fantasies, she slid from the rock after a careful look round, and moments later was hurriedly slipping into her clothes, ready to start for home.

By the time she came into sight of the house, the physical reaction to the snake was dissipated, but her mental reaction remained. She felt somehow betrayed, and vulnerable.

She also wondered, with growing anticipation, if Ben might have come back early after all. And how she would react to seeing him now that her feelings were so vividly evident.

Surely he wouldn't be able to see it? Or might he? She

would have to keep a tight rein on her emotions, for sure.

She rounded the corner of the yards and quickly halted at sight of the expensive car parked before the large verandah. It was an unexpected sight, not least because she knew of no visitors who should be coming today. Then she looked up into the shade of the verandah, where her father and Robyn were sitting with another couple, and felt a knot convulse in her stomach.

The snake had indeed been prophetic. Sitting there, large as life, were Ken and Kim Lee! But there wasn't a sign of Ben, which made it all the more surprising.

CHAPTER SEVEN

'Miss Lyle! How very nice to see you again,' smiled Ken Lee, advancing to the edge of the porch with hand outstretched.

His greeting was effusive, and genuinely friendly, Kate thought. But there was a mildly furtive look in his eye that made her wonder if he was truly certain of his own welcome. That was confirmed by the look Robyn shot her as she shook Ken's hand and then stepped up on to the verandah to greet his sister as well.

'Miss Lee . . . welcome to Kathryn Downs,' she said, forcing up a smile she didn't believe.

Kim Lee's smile, if anything, was even phonier than Kate's, and she returned the greeting with an abruptness that bordered on the rude.

'Kim was just saying that they were in the area, and decided to accept Ben's offer to spend a few days with us,' Robyn explained, the look in her eye showing Kate she didn't believe a word of it.

'Well, we've plenty of room,' Kate replied, wondering how long she would be forced to act as a buffer between the vocal Robyn and the decidedly high-nosed Oriental beauty. Clearly Robyn was not impressed, and Kate, while not very happy about the situation herself, could see a world-class slanging match developing if Robyn weren't curbed.

Kim Lee, on the other hand, seemed totally oblivious to the flimsiness of her welcome. Ken, to give him his due, seemed far more sensitive to the undercurrents, but Kate very much suspected that he was the follower in the sibling pair, and would set aside his own feelings to do what his sister wanted.

And at that moment it was very clear what Kim Lee wanted. 'Where is Ben . . . ton?' she asked in her musical voice. 'I would have expected him to be here. He is not . . . in Brisbane or somewhere?'

'Oh, he's gone off to town for something or other,' Robyn offered before Kate could interrupt. 'He said he might be back for tea, or he might not. I think maybe he's got a girl-friend stashed away somewhere.'

Kate almost laughed aloud at the sudden change in Kim Lee's face at that suggestion. The deeply-hooded eyes flickered like those of a snake, and petulant lines appeared around the rosebud mouth. Only for an instant; then Kim recovered and her voice was syrupy sweet in reply.

'Oh, I do not think so. I think he has . . . other interests.'

'And so have I,' said Henry Lyle, obviously glad of a chance to extricate himself from the tense situation. 'I've got some fencing to check, among other things. Want to come along, Ken, or would you rather wait with the ladies?'

'I have not seen your set-up here,' Ken said. 'I would be pleased to accompany you, if I might be allowed to change first?'

He, too, looked as if he would take any opportunity to get away. Kate wondered indeed that he had even worried about changing, despite the expensive business suit being hardly suitable for a trek round the farm.

'Of course; please forgive my bad manners,' she apologised instantly.

'Robyn, would you please make us some tea, and I'll show the Lees to their rooms.'

It took only a few minutes before Ken Lee, having apologetically refused tea, went off with Kate's father, leaving Kate and Robyn with the unwelcome task of entertaining his sister.

Kate, against her better judgment but in a dangerously go-for-broke mood, had put Kim in the room directly next to the one Ben used, with Ken one door farther away. As she watched the lovely raven-haired girl delicately sipping at her tea, it was a move she thought it likely she would regret.

Still, if Ben Croft was all that attracted to this particular Oriental doll, who was she to stand in his way? Great theory, Kate, she thought. But then why don't you really believe it?

It was only too obvious that Kim Lee had engineered this visit for one reason only—to see Ben Croft. And maybe, Kate thought, to spy out the ground as well. Certainly she wasn't one whit interested in making idle conversation with Kate and Robyn; that much was just too clear.

Pleading a headache, she retired to her room, leaving the other two girls with the task of preparing dinner. But at least it allowed them time to talk privately.

'Well, how's that for a surprise?' Robyn hissed. She was

busily peeling potatoes, working the paring knife with a vigour that made Kate worry for her fingers. 'How can you manage to be so damned civil?' Robyn continued savagely. 'I just cannot abide that snooty little bitch!'

'What can we do but be nice to her?' Kate replied with a shrug of her shoulders. 'She's Ben's guest, after all, and he does have a substantial share in the place.'

'Ben's *guest*!' Robyn snorted. 'She's her own guest, that one. Can you honestly imagine Ben inviting *anyone*, except in the most casual and general way, without letting you know first to expect them? No way!'

'Well, she's here now, so there's nothing to be done about it,' said Kate, wishing she dared allow herself such abject hostility but knowing she couldn't.

Ben's guest and you're welcome to her, she thought, and gained a ray of satisfaction when Ben telephoned just on five o'clock and she was able to inform him of his visitors before he could get round to telling her he wouldn't be back for dinner.

'The Lees? There?' The surprise in his voice surely couldn't be feigned, Kate thought, and suddenly felt decidedly better about the whole thing. He hadn't been expecting Kim Lee after all.

'Well, of course that changes things a bit,' he said then, dashing her good spirits. 'I'll be there in about an hour, if you can hold dinner that long.'

'Of course,' Kate replied. 'We hadn't planned dinner until seven, in any event, so don't hurry.' She sounded curt, and realised it when she heard his sharply indrawn breath.

'You don't have to worry about me, Kate,' he said then. 'I very seldom take chances, and never while driving.'

'It's hardly my business to worry about you, is it?' she snapped shrewishly, and immediately regretted it.

'That's what I love about you—your pleasant disposition,' he replied, and she could *see* him laughing at her. 'See you in an hour or so, and don't do anything rash until I get there,'

'I never do anything rash,' she replied haughtily, but he had already hung up.

Kim Lee's headache disappeared miraculously the instant Ben's vehicle halted in front of the house, and she was out on the verandah to greet him before he had turned off the ignition.

'All over him like a rash,' Robyn quipped drily, but Kate was far more interested in Ben's reaction to the diminutive beauty and the tight-fitting cheong-sam that revealed every detail of her lovely figure.

When she saw Ben lower his head to meet Kim's kiss, however, she turned away quickly at the sudden pain inside her, a pain that grew with the certainty she now felt about her own emotions.

'I'm not halfway in love with him,' she whispered to herself, and had to blink back the tears of reality. She was totally, completely, desperately in love with Ben Croft. And from his reaction to Kim Lee, he couldn't care less!

Well, to hell with him! This was her home, even more than his, and if he wanted to carry on his affair right before her nose he could damned well be discreet about it, Kate thought bitterly. At least she'd made it easy for him in her room allotment.

Not bothering to greet Ben herself, she remained in the kitchen while Robyn went home to change for dinner, then slipped unnoticed to her own room to change too.

But what to wear? She was half inclined to simply return in her usual jeans and T-shirt, but realised that her father, if no one else, might be either offended or curious at such a move. But she was determined not to be seen as competing with her *guest*, and in the end she chose a simple dress in burnt orange tones that complimented her increasing suntan without looking terribly ostentatious.

When she reached the lounge room, it was she who was surprised by the sudden uplifting of dress standards. Robyn had gone all out, arriving in basic black with just enough jewellery to set off her colouring, but it was the men who contributed most. Kate's father was tieless, but dressed in more than his usual style, and Bill Campbell looked as if he was set for a once-a-year night on the town, with slicked-back hair and a necktie that looked as if it would choke him.

Ken Lee had switched back to his dark business suit, or its twin, and his sister was radiant in a backless, sleeveless, almost topless creation of distinctly Oriental design.

It was only too obvious as well that Kim was the centre of masculine attention and loving every minute of it, manipulating her audience like an accomplished actress.

You've got style, sweetie, I have to admit it, Kate thought ruefully. Then she saw Ben as he stepped from the admiring throng and her eyes widened.

Where Kim had brought out vivid clothes sense in the other men, it seemed to have affected Ben very strangely indeed. He was wearing his oldest, most comfortable slacks and a sweater that Kate had privately, once, thought seriously about losing in the wash. Casual loafers and a shirt wide open at the throat contributed to his air of simply not being ready to upset his routine, even for visitors.

Very strange, Kate thought. It wasn't like Ben at all, but she had little opportunity to mull over it.

'Hello, Kate,' he said with a smile. 'Come and sit down and I'll bring you a drink. Everybody else is one ahead of you.'

'No, thanks, I'll get my own,' she demurred, subtly returning his attention to their guests. 'Is anyone else ready while I'm at it?'

'Oh, yes,' chimed Kim in her musical voice, but there was naked hostility, not music in those dark eyes as she handed Kate her glass with a distinct mistress-servant gesture.

Kate merely smiled graciously, her emotions held too strongly in check for Kim to have any effect at all. Ben's slightest look might turn her knees to water, but she was damned if his little concubine was going to get to her.

Moving in a daze of pent-up tension, she walked about the room slowly, almost blindly, talking to whomever she must, but almost entirely unaware of what she was saying, or what was said to her. She had one drink, then another, and was about to start on a third when Ben cornered her and took the glass from her hand in a gesture that looked extremely gentle but nearly broke one of her fingers.

'You'd better leave some room for the wine with dinner, Kate,' he said softly, and his tone brooked no argument.

'Whatever you say,' she acknowledged, and picked up the glass as soon as his back was turned. And he *knew*. Kate drained the glass and replaced it on the sideboard before Ben had crossed the room, but when he turned to look at her again his eyes were glittering, angry emeralds and his mouth was tightly drawn.

'Stiff cheese,' she muttered, and would have refilled the glass again but for Robyn dragging her into the kitchen to finish off dinner.

'Oh, that woman!' Robyn breathed once they were through the door. '*Ben . . . ton!* If I hear her say that once more I'm going to throw up—or throw something. I'm surprised you haven't, already. Or are you waiting until you're thoroughly smashed?'

'Oh, leave it, Robyn!' Kate snapped. 'I'm not drinking any more and it isn't worth discussing anyway. So just leave it.'

'Your funeral,' Robyn replied airily, and lapsed into silence as they got ready to serve the enormous saddle of venison she had so carefully prepared.

Dinner, astoundingly enough, was an enormous success. The venison was done to perfection, much enhanced by Robyn's extensive culinary art, and was accompanied by small, glazed carrots, roasted new potatoes, crisp beans and a lightly-dressed salad.

The presentation was visually excellent, drawing compliments even from Kim Lee, who Kate had feared might throw a pall on the affair with her superior attitude.

The slender Oriental was soon into a knowledgeable discussion with Robyn about haute cuisine, and Ben and brother Ken also became involved in the often heated but purely friendly debate.

Kate said very little, preferring to watch and listen in her role as hostess, although most of her attention was inadvertently focussed on Ben. She noticed, seemingly for the first time, the lines of his profile, the subtle contours of massive strength, solidarity. While evading his eyes, she nonetheless studied him thoroughly, memorising him into her soul.

If Kim's use of English was sometimes quaint, surely the result of an affectation now become habit, her brother had no such difficulty. He was a literate and consummate conversationalist, obviously a close and long-standing friend of Ben's, and once relaxed he showed himself to be highly entertaining as well.

The inequality of numbers had resulted in an unusual seating plan, with Kate at the head of the table, flanked by her father and Bill, then Robyn beside Kate's father,

Kim between Bill and Ben, and Ken Lee at the foot of the table.

From Kate's viewpoint it was perfect; Bill's habitual silence and her father's interest in Robyn kept the dinner conversation flowing away from her, rather than forcibly involving her. The position also left her free to attend to kitchen matters when they arose, without disturbing the flow of talk.

And when the meal itself was over, and everyone had returned to the lounge room for port and coffee, Kate felt equally free to slip away to the kitchen and begin washing up. Alone there with her inner thoughts, she plunged her hands into the soapy water and began the laborious process of reconciling her obviously wasted love for Ben.

'Hiding? That's not like you, Kate.' The voice slammed like a hammer into her silent communion, and she turned with a start.

'Here, I'll give you a hand with those,' said Ben, reaching down to grab the tea-towel.

'Don't bother,' she replied as calmly as she could. 'I seem to remember I owe you this, anyway. Please go back and entertain our guests.'

'*Our* guests? As I remember it, I had very little to do with it,' he replied with a suggestive lift of one dark eyebrow.

'Oh, don't be ridiculous!' she snapped, lifting a sudsy hand to pluck away the towel from his hand.

'Now who's being ridiculous?' he grinned, grabbing it back before Kate could move. 'Don't be so defensive, Kate, it doesn't agree with you.'

'And stop trying to tell me what's good for me,' she snapped, making a futile grab for the tea-towel. 'I'm perfectly capable of running my life without help or advice from you!'

'Ah, yes,' he agreed. 'But are you enjoying it?' And his eyes were mocking green orbs.

'I was until you came along,' she retorted, turning back to her work as if to ignore him. Wasted gesture; he didn't take the hint but only returned to his self-appointed drying task.

'Oh, sure. Kate . . . Lester, wasn't it? The merry widow. So merry she could barely wait until her husband was cold in the ground before changing back to her maiden name.'

His voice dripped sarcasm, and . . . was it contempt? Kate didn't bother to ask. She spun around to slash at him with her free hand, oblivious to the froth of suds that cascaded ahead of the blow. Ben pivoted neatly to avoid it.

'Temper, temper!' he cautioned. 'I might just hit you back, don't forget. And you're a bit vulnerable up to your elbows in water.'

'Why don't you just go . . . away!' she snarled. 'I'm sure there must be somebody else who'd welcome your attentions. I don't!'

'Why? Because I won't let you play the dominant feminist role? Really, Kate! You wouldn't enjoy it if I did.'

'Leave me alone,' she replied dully, refusing to rise to the bait. She stared straight ahead, focusing her eyes on her work.

'Poor dear Kate . . . you've had just so many hassles, haven't you?' his persuasive voice continued, and then butterfly fingers flickered across the nape of her neck, a faery's touch that sent shivers racing through her.

Kate's knees trembled, and the glass she was washing slipped from nerveless fingers to thunk softly against the steel bottom of the sink.

'Don't,' she whispered. 'Oh, please . . . don't.'

And he stopped. Or did he? His touch was so feather-light she couldn't be sure, and eventually she had to gather the courage to look over at him.

'Why did you lie to me, Kate?' he asked in a voice as soft as his touch, but much colder, like the breeze from an ice-floe.

Lie? What on earth was he talking about? And *why* couldn't he stop touching her, caressing her?

'About your husband,' he continued, 'about your marriage, if that's what you choose to call it.'

'I never . . .' she broke off quickly. What did he know? Even his fingers seemed icy now, and all pretence of washing dishes had ceased. 'What are you talking about?'

'I'm talking about you going to such lengths to convince me you were happily married, when instead your husband was nothing but a womanising little punk who made your life hell.'

'Says who?' she demanded, and feared the answer.

'Your father, among others. But since I could expect him to be prejudiced, I arranged . . . other opinions.'

'I don't think I know what you mean,' she replied cautiously. But she did know, and it frightened her.

'Oh, hell!' His voice was harsher now, showing an impatience, a frustration with her hedging. 'Kate, I'm an international businessman. I do have contacts—even in Melbourne.'

'You . . . checked up on me?' Her tone was incredulous, but her mind raced feverishly. Had he actually checked up on her? And did he now, then, know all about Wayne, Wayne's death, and that living hell of an inquest?

'Very discreetly,' he said in assuring tones that did nothing for her peace of mind. 'Enough to know what kind of person he was, what he was up to the night he died.'

'You . . . you . . . What *right* did you have to do such a thing?'

He shrugged. 'I wanted to know, and you wouldn't tell me. It's not important. What I want to know is why . . .'

'Not important? You use your influence to intrude on my privacy, to . . . to *investigate* me! And you say it's not important?' Kate blazed forth in the only emotion free to her—anger.

She jerked back from the kitchen counter and sink, twisting away from Ben's touch and swivelling round to face him from several steps away.

'I think you are the most . . . most contemptible creature I've ever met,' she snarled. 'Just . . . just because I didn't fall down at your feet or go all mushy when you smiled, your little ego's been hurt. And of course it couldn't be your fault, could it? My God!'

She shivered inside, but now the shudder was because of the rage that boiled up, bringing with it only the desire to strike out, to hurt.

'Poor little Ben,' she sneered. 'Couldn't have his own way, so he sulked. Couldn't understand why this obviously available widow wouldn't turn out to be an easy roll in the hay, so he called in the troops and had her investigated. What did you expect, that I'd be so desperate after three months alone that I'd be begging for it?

'Well, let me tell you something, Mr irresistible *Ben* . . . *ton* Croft. It wasn't just three months; it was a lot longer than three months—and I had a lot better offers than any you could make. And turned them down. And you have the audacity to criticise Wayne! At least he didn't have to sneak around behind my back to get me into bed with him!'

She paused then, fighting for breath, for control, for her very existence, it seemed. But when he opened his mouth to reply she shouted him down.

'Don't you say one word! I've heard everything from

you I ever want to as long as I live. You're nothing to me—you never were and you never will be. I wouldn't have you if you were the last man alive, you underhanded, cowardly, sneaking . . . scum! Is that clear?'

He stood silent, eyes like pale green caves of ice, his jaw clenched and his posture rigid as if he were carved from stone. For years, it seemed, he stood there, until a voice from the doorway interrupted.

'Ben . . . ton? Ah, here you are. I thought you promised to take me for a walk,' said Kim Lee, slinking into the room with absolutely no conception of what she was interrupting.

'Oh, I am sorry,' she said then. 'I didn't realise I was interrupting something.' The syrupy voice intimated otherwise, but neither Ben nor Kate seemed to notice.

'Very clear,' he said in a voice from the grave. 'Yes, I'm sorry, love; I was going to give Kate a hand first, but it seems she prefers to work alone.' He dropped the tea towel on the counter as if it were something soiled and turned away quickly to sling his arm round Kim's tiny waist. 'Come on, my little fortune cookie. We'll go look at the stars and see if they have any message for us.'

Kate stood, struggling against her tears until they had truly gone, then found to her surprise that there were no tears . . . only a vast, yawning emptiness. A cold place, damp and dark and horrible.

She turned and plunged her hands into the warmth of the dishwater, trying to get enough warmth inside her so that she could start building a wall around where her heart had been.

By the time Robyn walked in, saying, 'Is this where you've been? Oh, Kate, this could have waited,' the wall was in place, shaky and roughly cobbled together, but able to hold the tears and the freezing emptiness.

'I just thought I'd get a start on these dishes,' Kate replied lightly. 'It's no trouble.'

'I thought Ben came through this way,' Robyn said then, a suspicious gleam in her eye.

Kate ignored subtlety. 'He's out walking with Kim Lee,' she replied directly, and was proud that her voice didn't even quiver.

'I . . . see,' said Robyn. But she didn't see. She couldn't, wouldn't ever be allowed to. No one would. 'Well, you'd better come back in and help with the entertaining. Everybody's wondering where you'd got to.' She paused fractionally. 'If you're up to it, that is . . .'

'Well, why shouldn't I be?' Kate laughed shrilly. 'It was just that I didn't want to drink any more, and—well, I was a bit bored with the conversation.'

'You should have stayed,' said Robyn. 'Kim Lee's not half as bad as she seems, once she lets go a bit—and her brother's absolutely a riot. I quite like him.'

'So do I,' Kate replied, truthfully enough, and she meekly followed Robyn back to the lounge room, joining gamely in the conversation and forcing herself not to watch the door for Ben's return.

As soon as he did return, with his decorative companion looking thoroughly kissed, Kate made her excuses and retired to her room. She didn't think about the unfinished dishes, or even her earlier anger, now hardened to a kind of hatred. She undressed and flung herself into bed without a thought of Ben Croft, but his eyes haunted her dreams when she finally slept.

Morning came within minutes, it seemed, bringing with it the savage truth of the term *cold grey light of dawn* and bringing Kate sleepily awake with the fear that she'd be late to join Ben in patrolling the fence. Then she came properly awake and sank back into her pillow with a disgusted sigh.

Let him take his little fortune cookie, she thought. And wished that he *would* take Kim Lee—take her and go away from Kathryn Downs, never, ever to return.

But that, Kate realised, was at best unrealistic. If anyone would have to leave Kathryn Downs, it would be herself! Ben Croft was a major partner in the deer farm undertaking; she was merely an appendage, especially now that it appeared her father's health was improving and Robyn might be the woman who would be looking after him in any event.

So be it, she thought savagely, although something inside her twisted at the thought of having to leave this idyllic place. She realised—too late?—that even her professed desire to find a job had been only a ploy to aid her in resisting Ben, to help create the required illusion of independence.

But to stay, now, would be a gesture of utter foolishness. Regardless of the fact that Ben couldn't—didn't—love her, they shared a strong physical attraction that would sooner or later explode if they continued to be thrown together.

And she would be the one to be hurt, to be used as a convenience and then discarded, or at best kept for his next visit, an appendage of the spare bedroom.

'Never!' she vowed aloud.

Kate purposely waited in bed, one eye on the window that allowed her a view of the track Ben must take on his patrol, until she saw his tall, lithe figure striding away from the yards. Only then did she rise, wash and dress in her habitual jeans and shirt.

She arrived in the kitchen to find a single, fresh-washed coffee cup on the drainboard and a pot of still-hot coffee on the counter. She poured herself some, quickly made some toast and jam, and settled down to eat before the rest of the house was awake.

Robyn arrived just as Kate was finishing, and together they put together the large farm breakfast which Kate's father, Bill and Ben would be expecting in less than an hour.

'I wonder if we'll have our guests for breakfast this early,' Robyn mused. 'Not likely, considering how late we stayed up last night. Everybody but you, that is; I hope we didn't keep you awake.'

'No, I slept remarkably well,' Kate lied. Although it hadn't been the party downstairs that had kept her from sleeping, really. Only one member of it.

'What are the plans for today?' Kate asked Robyn casually, already thinking of her own intention to avoid Ben Croft at any cost. She might, she decided, manufacture an excuse to go to town, or perhaps simply slip away to her sunbathing pool for as long as she could reasonably absent herself from the house.

'Nothing special. I think Ben's taking Kim on a guided tour with her brother, but there's nothing else on that I've heard about.'

'You wouldn't mind, then, if I didn't hang around?' said Kate. 'I was thinking I might go to town.'

'Oh, couldn't you put it off until tomorrow?' Robyn looked slightly perturbed. 'I have to go in then anyway, and we could go together.'

'Sure ... why not? It isn't that important that I go today. I'll wander up and have a swim instead.'

Robyn gazed at her speculatively. 'Avoiding someone?'

'Avoiding everyone. I think I've got too used to the solitude here,' Kate replied. 'Even with only three people extra, I feel sort of ... crowded.'

It was a dubious excuse at best, but Robyn didn't comment on it. Instead she merely looked at Kate as if trying to see without asking what might be wrong.

'Oh, don't look at me like that,' Kate blustered. 'I . . . I just feel that I have some serious thinking to do, and I'd rather do it . . . alone, that's all.'

'Don't be so defensive,' Robyn replied calmly, and it was so typically a Ben comment that Kate flinched, though not outwardly.

Fortunately Bill Campbell arrived then, effectively halting that aspect of the conversation, and a moment later Henry Lyle walked into the kitchen with a cheery greeting for everyone.

Instant decision! 'Dad, do you suppose I could talk to you a moment . . . right after breakfast?'

He looked at her, only mildly curious. 'Of course, Kate.' And, luckily, not a single question. Not until later, when they would be assured of privacy. And yet he did look . . . speculative?

'Don't look so bothered; it's nothing serious,' she said as she left the room. The worst of the work was done and Kate could cope now without having to face Ben. Robyn would handle the rest.

When her father entered the study half an hour later, carrying a tray with coffee for both of them, Kate rose from her chair to take it from him. 'Here, I'll pour,' she said, 'you always spill it.'

'Ah,' he mused, then looked squarely into her dark eyes. 'Let's have it, Kate. You're not fooling anybody, especially not your old dad.'

'Well . . . I've been thinking I should be leaving soon,' she began lamely. 'I . . . I mean, I can't stay here for ever; there's just no need for it and there isn't enough for me to do. You don't need two women here to look after you. And I wouldn't go as far as Melbourne, this time. Just Nambour, if I can organise something there. Or Brisbane;

that's only a couple of hours away.'

'I see.' He didn't, she realised, but was using the expression to try and force her to elaborate. His tired eyes seemed to stare straight into her soul, but he was kind enough not to probe harshly.

'Yes, I suppose it must be pretty boring out here after the city,' he said then.

'Oh, no,' she protested, 'it isn't that, not at all. I love it here, honestly. It's just that I don't feel I'm pulling my weight. There just isn't enough for me to do that seems . . . well, relevant. It doesn't take the two of us to handle the cooking and cleaning, and—well . . .'

'I don't suppose Robyn has anything to do with this? Or should I say, Robyn and I?' The implications were obvious.

'I couldn't be happier for both of you,' she said honestly. 'And no, it isn't a matter of feeling that I'm in the way of anything, or . . . well, you know.'

'I wish I did,' he sighed. 'But you're a big girl now, and you've got to find your own way, I suppose. It's just that I had rather hoped this could be a home for you, as it is for me, now.'

'Oh, but it will be,' she smiled. 'Definitely. I promise. That's why I don't want to move too far away, so I can come home at weekends, or holidays.'

'Or whenever Ben's not here?' His eyes glinted; Henry Lyle had lost none of his powers of observation.

'That's part of it, I suppose,' Kate replied stubbornly. In for a penny . . . 'We don't really get along too well, as I suppose you've noticed.'

'Oh yes. Especially since Madam Butterfly arrived. I must say, Kate, that I never expected to see my own daughter so consumed by jealousy and her own ego that . . . well, I'm not going to lecture you. Do as you must.'

'Now just a minute,' protested Kate. 'You can't just make a comment like that and then drop it without some explanation. What do you mean about my ego?'

'I'm glad to see you're not disputing the jealousy bit,' he said rather drily. 'And as for your ego, let's just say you've made a rather extreme transition from being over-dominated to over-liberated. When you arrived here you were still weathering the effects of Wayne's death, and that's fair enough, I suppose. But lately you've simply been letting your fear of Ben's strength colour your reactions to the point of ridiculousness. Personally, I'm surprised he bothers with you at all; I certainly wouldn't.'

'Well, you could hardly call Robyn submissive,' she said angrily, trying to cover her confusion with an offensive attack.

'Certainly not! But then Robyn's totally certain of who she is, both as a woman and as a person. You, my dear, are not! Or if you are you do a damned poor job of displaying it.'

'That's not true! Just because I can't get along with Ben Croft, especially with everybody pushing me at him, there's no reason for you to say things like that,' Kate raged.

'If you can't get along with him, it's because you're too busy trying to maintain your independence,' her father said. 'And you're too blind to see that you're trying to defend something that's never been at risk in the first place. You're not a child any more, Kate, but for some reason you've got yourself hung up on playing a role that doesn't even fit you. You've forgotten how to be yourself.'

You've forgotten how to be yourself. Kate dissected that remark as she strolled slowly along the path to her pool. Could it really be true?

Of course not, she thought, and then wasn't quite so sure. There was no arguing the fact that contact with Ben somehow brought out a strongly aggressive aspect of her personality, but she was beginning to wonder if it wasn't merely an instinctive or subconscious attempt to deny his attraction. Or was she still reacting to Wayne's death, to her own guilt? That seemed less than likely, since apart from Ben's mention of it, she hadn't so much as thought about her short-lived and horrendous marriage in weeks.

Now she did, and wasn't particularly surprised to find that with her guilt no longer the overriding influence, it was like looking back through a very hazy window. Of course there were distinct memories, both good and bad, but most of that period of her life was now more dreamlike than anything. It was as if it had happened to somebody else.

Difficult, even, to reconstruct Wayne's face, although Ben Croft's rugged features formed without any difficulty in her mind's eye.

Ben Croft! Truly the answer to a widow's prayer, except that his interests were obviously too well catered for by Kim Lee for Kate to have any chance.

If only she could simply forget him! But how, when he was such an integral part of her life already? Even if she were to leave Kathryn Downs as she planned, Ben would still hover over the place like a ghost waiting for her return.

But at least, she thought, she wouldn't be constantly reminded of him, seeing his presence, his influence, if she were working somewhere else.

Kate thought more about the problem during her swim, but it wasn't much closer to resolution when a bank of dark clouds swept over the ridge to shut off her sun and bring a chill to the small glade.

The rain started before she was a quarter of the way home, and by the time she reached the house she was soaked to the skin and shivering with cold. Her hair was

plastered down and dripping and her shirt was pasted to
her body when she slithered her way across the deer yards
and rushed in a final dash for the porch.

'Are you all right?' Ben's question caught her by surprise
as she leapt up the steps to find him standing there, lost in
the shadow of his heavy oilskins.

'Yes,' she gasped. 'Just wet, that's all. And . . . cold.'

'I should damn well think so. Where the hell have you
been, anyway?'

'Swimming . . . up there,' she replied with a vague wave
behind her. 'Now if you'll excuse me, I'm going to have a
hot shower before I shiver to death.'

'Right! And put on something warm when you're done.
I'll fix you a hot toddy while you're showering,' he said,
reaching out to open the door for her.

Kate was too busy dashing up the stairway to voice a
reply, but the gesture surprised her just a bit. After her
treatment of him the night before, she thought, it was
more than generous.

Ben was waiting for her in the kitchen when she finally
finished showering, and had wrapped up well in a fluffy
towelling robe and warm slippers. With her hair only
towelled dry and gathered into a damp ponytail, Kate felt
she looked about fifteen, but there was nothing childish
about the drink she was handed.

She gasped as the warm liquor clawed its way down her
throat to nestle then like a live coal in her stomach.
'Heavens! What have you put in this?' she cried once she
had got her breath back.

'Medicine. Drink it all and you may never be cold
again,' he grinned. 'Can't have you down with a cold for
the wedding.'

'Wedding? What are you talking about?' she asked with
a shake of her head. 'Whose wedding?'

'Well, whose do you think?' he replied with a smug, infuriating grin.

'You mean, you and . . .' Kate couldn't force out the name. A stab of dismay thrust up from inside her to pinion her tongue.

'Me? Don't be ridiculous,' he snorted. 'If you were going to be at *my* wedding, dear Kate, there'd be more to worry about than just having a cold.'

'Well, thank you very much!'

He shrugged. 'It was a compliment, although I wouldn't expect you to recognise it. And while I wouldn't be upset if you snuffled through my wedding ceremony, your old dad might not be so charitable.'

CHAPTER EIGHT

'DAD? And Robyn? Oh, how wonderful!' she cried. 'But, what's happened? I mean, Dad didn't mention anything to me this morning . . . and now you . . .'

'Settle down,' he said calmly. 'He probably didn't mention it this morning because he hadn't asked her yet. I'm a bit in the dark myself, actually. First I heard was when they decided to roar off to town to make the arrangements or check on the church, or whatever. Our guests went along for the ride, or to do some shopping, I'm not sure which.'

'I see,' said Kate. 'But you didn't go.'

'Obviously. And just as well, or you'd have had nobody to mix your toddy,' he said. 'I'd have come and scrubbed your back for you, too, but you didn't give me a chance to ask.'

'I should hope not!' retorted Kate, fighting down the vivid images *that* created in her mind. 'I'm quite capable of washing my own back, thank you.'

'Or too independent to recognise a purely friendly gesture when you meet it,' he chuckled. 'What's the matter . . . afraid I'd be overwhelmed by your feminine charms?'

'When will they be back, do you think?' Kate asked in a deliberate change of subject. There was simply no way she was going to allow Ben Croft to get her goat now. She wanted to revel in the pleasure of the coming marriage, not torture herself with sexual sparring.

'Probably for dinner,' he replied absently. 'Speaking of which, I think you and I had better put our heads together and come up with something super-special. It'll be a bit tricky to match last night's feast, but left-over venison is hardly what I'd call an appropriate dinner for such an occasion.'

'Certainly not,' Kate agreed. 'But I don't know what we can come up with on such short notice.'

'That's because you haven't the proper faith,' he said. 'How about roast quail, baby potatoes and some kind of fancy salad? Oh, and a cake, of course. You can make that.'

'And you're going to do the rest? This I just have to see,' Kate retorted, her caution forgotten. 'When I arrived you were complaining about having to live on your own cooking, and now you want to be super-chef!'

'Just don't get in my way,' he replied. 'And try watching; you might learn something.'

He scrubbed up quickly, spent several minutes scrounging round in the bottom of the deep-freeze to emerge with a dozen quail, then got busy mixing an incredible stuffing for the tiny birds.

Kate sat and watched as he chopped onion expertly, used a wide variety of spices with the discretionary touch of long experience, and within half an hour had his entire production ready for the eventual thawing of the birds.

'Right! Kitchen's yours now,' he said with a superior smirk. 'And see that your cake is as good as my efforts, eh?'

'I'm tempted to let you make the cake as well,' she retorted. 'You've been deliberately misleading me about your abilities.'

'Only because I'm a rotten, conniving, devious sort,' he said. 'As well as underhanded, cowardly and sneaky, of course.'

Kate flushed. Words spoken in anger, but apparently not so easily forgotten by Ben as by herself. The thought that he had so deliberately sought information from her past still rankled, but her thoughts during the day had brought with them a small realisation that she could as easily be complimented by his interest. At the very least she wasn't going to let that argument flare up again.

'I . . . suppose I was a bit harsh,' she admitted. 'But it just made me so angry at the time that . . . I . . .'

'And I probably deserved it,' he said. 'Not for what I did; when I want to know something I generally manage it. But thinking back I must admit it couldn't have been the most gentle way of telling you about it.'

'It was . . . a bit shocking,' she admitted. And then, to try and avoid further discussion about it, 'Why did you let me believe you couldn't cook very well?'

'It was one way of making you feel needed, and I had the feeling you might need that under the circumstances.'

And now it's no longer necessary, Kate thought. Because Father's taken care of, and it doesn't matter any more if I stay or go. The words popped into her mouth: 'I'll be leaving soon. Did Dad mention it to you?'

'No, but I'm not surprised,' he said, starting to gather the ingredients for the cake. Obviously he was taking her at her word and would bake it himself. 'You seem to have recovered fairly well from your ordeal now, and I suppose you miss the bright lights.'

'Not particularly,' said Kate. 'But I do have to find something to justify my existence, and now that Robyn's here permanently I'll have to strike out on my own again. Two cooks in one kitchen is at least one too many. And besides, she's much better at it than I.'

'So what are you going to do, or have you decided yet?' His tone was casually curious.

'Oh, I don't know. See if I can find some sort of teaching job, I suppose, although I don't know if there's a place for an economics instructor in Nambour, and I'd rather stay there than in Brisbane.'

'Why not come to work for me?' He said it so quietly Kate wasn't at first certain she had heard him right.

'For . . . for you?' she stammered, dreading to hear the question repeated. How could she possibly find a diplomatic way out of this? She couldn't possibly go to work for Benton Croft. It would defeat the whole purpose of her leaving in the first place. 'I don't have any skills that would qualify,' she added hastily. 'I'm a teacher, not a practical economist.'

'Oh, I think you'd qualify all right,' he replied, but whatever else he planned to say was lost in the timely arrival of the Lees and the newly engaged couple.

Kate flew to the door to meet them, forgetful of her rather unconventional dress, and surrounded both her father and Robyn with hugs and kisses as she wildly congratulated them and told them how pleased she was.

'But you should have told me this morning,' she said in mock anger.

'Don't you try and bully me, Kate,' her father replied with a fond grin. 'There's somebody else to do that now. I would have told you, actually, but if you'll recall we had other things to discuss.' He held her off at arm's length, eyes raking over her pony tail, robe and slippers. 'And what in God's green earth have you been up to while we were gone? You look . . . well . . .'

'Oh,' said Kate, suddenly conscious of how she must look not only to her father, but to their guests, 'I got caught in the storm and Ben . . . well, I had to have a shower, and . . .' She broke it off there, realising that every word made the thing sound worse.

Robyn was laughing delightedly, but Kim Lee was shooting daggers from her dark eyes, while Henry Lyle merely appeared vaguely confused about it all.

Ben's appearance at the kitchen door, an apron snugged around his lean waist, drew some of the interest from Kate, until he said laconically, 'We've been playing house, sort of, only I got stuck in the kitchen.'

That brought a scream of laughter from Robyn and another dirty look from Kim, but at least it broke the growing tension Kate felt inside because of the appearance of things.

'Oh lord, I knew we should have eaten in town,' Henry Lyle sighed. 'I'd suggest going straight back, but the weather's against us. It's not fit for man nor beast outside. Did you at least supervise, Kate? Or are we forced to endure whatever this maniac provides?'

'Well, there's a fair bit of cold venison, anyway,' she replied with a grin. 'So we won't starve.'

'You won't,' Ben said forcefully. 'But you may be forced into a public apology—both of you—when you taste the glorious creation I've concocted. Now why don't you all trot off to the lounge while Kate gets herself dressed and I attend to my creative genius.'

Whereupon he returned to the kitchen while Kate
scurried up the staircase and into her room. Truly, she
thought, staring into her mirror, Ben seemed determined
to create the most favourable impressions. Playing house,
indeed! And to say it in front of her father with that cat-
that-ate-the-cream expression on his face . . . no wonder
Kim was upset!

She wondered, then, if Ben might be deliberately using
her to create a bit of honest jealousy in his volatile little
girl-friend. It seemed a ludicrous thing to do, and yet the
looks Kim had shot at Kate indicated that he might well
be succeeding.

'But why?' she asked her image. And then with a rueful
grin, 'Probably just to stir up a little excitement. I wouldn't
put anything past him.'

Where the evening before Kate had deliberately chosen
to subdue her appearance, some perverse instinct tonight
made her choose a flowing caftan in subtle apricot tones
that highlighted her colouring and, although warm, had a
distinctly sensual air through being slit to mid-thigh and
having a cunningly-cut neck and shoulder line that tended
to reveal considerable cleavage and shoulder.

She dabbed on only a bit of her favourite perfume, kept
her make-up to the barest minimum, and could do nothing
with her freshly-washed hair but let it hang in flowing
tresses over her shoulders.

As she stepped out on to the broad staircase, an
enhanced awareness gave her added height and presence,
which was much improved by Ben's frankly admiring
glance from the foot of the stairs.

'Very nice,' he murmured, taking her hand and leading
her graciously into the lounge room. Kate felt a swirl of
pleasure at his attentions, one which wasn't in the least

disturbed when he escorted Kim Lee into the room a few minutes later.

Something about her relationship with Ben had changed, Kate decided, and although she couldn't determine exactly what was different, she liked it. Definitely!

And this evening he had taken a great deal of care with his own appearance, with a glowing white dinner jacket over dark trousers and a neatly-tied bow-tie.

The dinner he had prepared was excellent, so much so that Robyn twitted him about making somebody a fine wife some day, a line that drew only a faintly cynical grin from Ben amidst howls of laughter from everyone else.

'Just so you remember that I'm not doing the washing up,' he said. 'Great chefs shouldn't have to, especially in a house with so many capable women.'

Kim Lee, surprisingly, picked up the cue immediately. 'Ah, but Robyn cannot be washing dishes tonight; it is her party,' she said quickly. 'So it will be the work of Kate only, except that of course I shall help her.'

Condescending little bitch, Kate thought. I can just imagine how much help you'll be. Easier to do it myself.

'Oh, no,' Ben replied. 'Don't forget that Kate cleaned up after last night's feast, which she also helped cook. Not quite in accordance with the rules, but what's done is done. Sorry, Kim, but tonight's all yours. Just think of it as good training for when you get married.'

Kim blanched, obviously as surprised by the order as was Kate, but it was Kate who spoke up before the dark-eyed Oriental beauty could say a word.

'Don't be ridiculous, Ben,' she snapped. 'I'll have no guest in my house conscripted into the kitchen like that, so just stop your teasing. If Kim wants to help, she's welcome, but only if *she* wants to.'

Ben shrugged, his eyes unreadable. 'Your house . . . your

rules,' he said, and dropped the subject like a lump of lead.

It took a few minutes to regain the festive spirit of the evening after that, but it seemed only Kate was really upset by his dictatorial comments. Certainly whatever tension might have existed disappeared when he slipped away to the kitchen and returned with an enormous, three-layered chocolate cake smothered in pale lime-green icing.

'No candles, I'm afraid,' he said, 'but I couldn't have figured out how to arrange them if we'd had some.'

Instead, Kate noticed when he set the cake down in the middle of the table, he had used grated chocolate to form a large heart atop the cake with her father's and Robyn's initials in the centre.

'Now, before anybody lays a finger on this, I want a definite announcement on the date for this auspicious occasion,' he said, 'because if it's too far in the future I just may take back the cake and save it for later.'

On being told the big day was during the Queensland Labour Day long weekend, barely a month away, he voiced his pleasure and gravely toasted the newly-engaged couple.

It wasn't until they were into the coffee and liqueurs, however, that he dropped his bombshell into Kate's future plans.

'I guess we'll have to forget about a job for you until some time in July, Kate,' he said casually. 'Somebody'll have to stay and look after Bill and me while these two are off on their honeymoon.'

Kate's first reaction was to protest. The last thing she wanted was to be forced into spending almost three more months in close proximity to Ben. But one glance at her father's face and she realised there wasn't any choice in the matter.

'Am I to presume this rule about cooking and washing

up will apply?' she asked. 'If so, I accept.'

Ben laughed. 'The way you cook, I'll gladly clean up after you,' he replied. 'And the timing will work out just right, too. I've got an idea about a job for you, but it may take that long to arrange.'

'Perhaps I'd be better finding my own job,' Kate demurred, hoping desperately that he would take the hint. No such luck!

'Oh, this one would be better than anything you'd be likely to come up with,' he replied gravely. And then, maddeningly, refused to give her the slightest hint about what he had in mind.

The rest of the evening, however, maintained a party atmosphere that made it difficult for Kate to concentrate on Ben's curious behaviour. He put on some dance music and insisted on starting off the dancing himself, with Kate as his partner.

It was a sweet combination of heaven and hell, she thought, floating in his arms to the slowest of waltzes and wishing the music would never end. Then, when it did, she found herself whirled into a faster number by her father, moving so swiftly she caught only fleeting glimpses of Ben holding Kim where she herself should have been.

Kate danced with all the men, finding to her surprise that the shy, silent Bill Campbell was an excellent and graceful partner while Ken Lee, with all his natural grace, wasn't much of a dancer at all.

At the first reasonable opportunity, however, she slipped discreetly away to the kitchen to begin the washing up and try to sort out her own thoughts and feelings.

There was surprisingly little to be done; obviously Ben was the type of cook that cleaned up as he went along, and only the actual dinner dishes required much attention from Kate. She was almost finished, indeed, when Kim Lee flashed into the room with a distinctly malignant gleam in her eye.

'Hah!' she said sibilantly. 'I should have known you would do this. Now Ben . . . ton will think that I deliberately avoided helping you, causing me to lose face, perhaps.' Then she recovered herself and shrugged complacently. 'Still, it does not matter. Domestic drudgery will not help you to trap Ben . . . ton into marriage. He needs . . . other things in a woman than that. I do not think you are much of a threat.'

And without waiting for a reply, she flounced back out the door, leaving Kate standing open-mouthed at the sink.

For an instant Kate had to resist a frightening urge to follow the other woman and slap her silly, but then her logic intervened. What was the sense? It could accomplish nothing since Kim had already cut her out of the running, though Kim didn't seem to know it. Pride, if nothing else, demanded that Kate ignore her rudeness. Bad enough to love Ben, without lowering herself to Kim's standards.

But later that night, lying sleepless as thunder raged about the rooftop and sheets of lightning flared across the night sky, Kate wondered if she were doing the right thing by accepting Ben's friendship. Certainly it was preferable to continuing the hostility she had begun, but it was also infinitely more dangerous, since it left her more vulnerable.

And to go to work for him—that was surely folly. But just how she would get out of it, she couldn't imagine. Unless, somehow, she could manage to find a job for herself before this thing he was considering could be organised . . . she would have to try, even at the risk of upsetting her father in the process.

She was still puzzling it over when sleep finally claimed her, a deep, sodden sleep undisturbed by the crashing weather outside. Morning arrived without sun, without any change in the continuous downpour that turned every piece of open ground to a boggy quagmire, treacherous underfoot and unstable.

'We've got problems,' Bill Campbell announced as Kate scampered down the stairs to find both him and Ben divesting themselves of dripping oilskins and mud-clumped boots.

'What is it?' she asked, immediately struck by the obvious concern on their faces. Both men had risen early— much more so than usual—to have completed their patrol this soon.

'Coffee, first,' Ben replied. 'And while we're having it perhaps you'd get everybody up and mobile. We're going to need every set of hands we've got.'

Kate did as she was told without further questions, and by the time the coffee was ready everyone had been mustered to the kitchen in various states of readiness. Robyn and Kate's father, along with Kate herself and Ken Lee, were dressed in well-worn jeans and shirts, while Kim arrived in a skimpy nightgown and robe that did little to hide her figure.

'Oh, for God's sake,' Ben snapped, 'go and get into something useful, Kim. You'd look a bit damn silly running around a paddock like that!'

To her immediate and petulant reply that she had nothing suitable, he muffled a curse and then asked Robyn to try and find something of hers for Kim to wear.

'And hurry it up, please, Robyn. We've not got a lot of time,' he said. 'The damned rain's brought a gully-washer and knocked out one whole section of fencing. The stag herd in the bottom paddock has got into the one farther up from them, and if we can't get them separated fairly quickly there'll be the most almighty ruckus once they start squaring up over the hinds.'

While Robyn scurried off to find the clothing and Kate busied herself making toast to accompany the coffee, Ben and Bill sat with the other two men, labouring over plans to separate the two herds with minimum fuss and worry.

'We'll have to try and manoeuvre the stag herd into number five paddock, even if it means taking a few risks,' said Ben. 'The girls should be able to handle the gates.'

'You'll have the devil to pay with that one antlered stag,' Henry Lyle warned. 'He's been stroppy enough with only one other stag to keep him busy; with the whole herd there he'll be ready to strike out at anything that moves.'

'Well, we'll just have to do what we can,' Ben replied. 'But I think we'll take a rifle just in case. I'd really hate to shoot the old devil, he's got such a magnificent rack, but we can't take too many chances with the other stags who will try and fight even if they haven't any antlers.'

It was a dismal procession that eventually made its way through the sodden grass of the transit paddocks to where a large log had smashed out the fencing in two areas where a gully sprawled through the paddocks. In dry weather, these gully fences presented no difficulties, but the heavy rains had washed out a dead tree that had become a mobile battering ram on its way down with the fast-flowing water.

'My fault,' Bill Campbell mourned at the sight. 'I noticed that damned tree a week ago and meant to lop it down, but then something came up and I forgot about it.'

'No sense worrying about blame now,' said Ben. 'I saw it too, and I imagine Henry did as well. The problem now is to get that fencing repaired and then start sorting out these deer.'

With everyone helping, they managed to shift the log and eventually achieved temporary but acceptable repairs to the fences, although further work would be needed, Ben said, once the weather allowed them to get machinery into the site.

That was the easy part. The rest was far from easy. The huge red stag, until that morning penned with his harem of hinds and a single, much younger stag to keep him on his most productive behaviour, was fairly livid at the invasion of his territory by more than a dozen other stags, each of them now intent on separating the hinds to form harems of their own.

Even without antlers, they were an imposing sight as they pranced and danced in preliminary mating battles among themselves, but it appeared that as yet none had worked up the nerve to challenge the doughty old warrior.

Led by Ben, the men quickly sized up the situation, and decided to first attempt shifting the stag herd through gates at either end of the paddock. Robyn was posted at one gate, leading away from the transit lanes to a disused paddock, while Kate and Kim were asked to handle the other paddock gate and one farther down that led from the transit lane to the paddock the stag herd had originally been in.

'It just may be that the old stag and his harem will come out, instead of the stag herd,' Ben warned them. 'It doesn't matter, one way or the other, so long as the two groups are separated, so if it happens, just get the gate shut and let them go.'

Kate nodded her understanding, hoping the fear she felt wouldn't show on her face. She remembered only too well the time that same giant stag had tried to skewer her with its antlers, and hoped this time she wouldn't have to be close enough for anything like a repeat performance.

She controlled a shiver as the four men moved into the paddock, each armed with a stout cudgel in case of attack.

Moving with infinite slowness, so as not to spook the wary deer more than necessary, they drifted towards the stags which were clumped closely together at one edge of the resident herd.

At first, it appeared the entire operation was going to be a case of beginner's luck. The stag herd began to move slowly away from the pawing, snorting monarch and his harem, easing indirectly towards the open gate where Robyn waited.

But the old stag obviously wanted no interference from either man or his own species. As the line of men drew abreast of him, he charged in towards them with a bellow of incoherent rage, shaking his antlers and flinging ropes of saliva with every motion of his head.

The line converged to drive him back, and the other stags immediately stopped their forward momentum and began to circle back towards the flanks of the harem.

Immediately the old stag abandoned his attack on the men and began a circle of his own to cut off the invaders, but the men had lost their first round; the stags were now moving away from the gate instead of towards it.

At Ben's direction, the men reformed their line and began another slow, steady approach, this time towards the stags and Kate's gate, which was closest. And once again it appeared the ruse would be successful.

Kate stood immobile, knowing that her slightest movement would be noticed by the stags, but that if she stayed utterly still they would be unlikely to notice her at all in her camouflaged position behind the brush flanking the gate.

Slowly they inched towards her, occasionally pausing while one stag or another threw back his head to scream out a roar of challenge to the frenzied monarch and his harem. The line of men now separated the two herds, and the stags were only steps from the gate.

The first was through, then the second, rearing to trumpet his defiance back into the paddock. And then, slowly, the others, and she could begin to haul in the rope that would pull the gate shut behind them.

The gate was nearly shut when Ben reached her position, and he flashed her a victorious thumbs-up sign and a mighty grin as he slipped through the narrow opening to follow the stag herd down the transit paddock towards Kim's position.

Kate, stiff from her long immobility and the tension of the exercise, moved slowly towards the gate as Ben and the stag herd drifted down the corridor between the paddocks and the rest of the men moved back along the fence to join Robyn at the far gate. They would return by a roundabout route, but Kate would follow Ben once the stags were turned out into their own paddock.

She closed the gate behind her, slipping the chain latch firmly in place, and was half turned around when the faint scream reached her ears.

The stags! Obviously spooked by some movement of Kim's, the entire herd was plunging back down the transit corridor, a seething mass of deer with flashing, razor-sharp hooves surging straight towards her. But before them—Ben!

With his back to the herd he was screaming something Kate couldn't hear, but his motions were like print. Climb up, up the gate, quickly.

Kate turned, waving her understanding as she grabbed at the first strand of wire she could reach, but even as she did so she saw the first of the deer reach Ben's position, saw flying hooves as the enormous animal plunged straight at him, through him, and Ben was a huddled figure on the muddy ground as the rest of the animals stampeded over him. She screamed, and the startled animals stopped, milling between herself and Ben.

Fear—fear for Ben, rather than herself—lent wings to her feet, then. Ignoring the milling stags, she sped up the corridor, passing so close to them that she could smell the excitement of their pungent, rutting aggression, the heat of their breath as they shifted and swung aside to give her passage. Once or twice she actually touched a brittle-haired flank in passing, but her eyes never left the still, oilskin-shrouded figure on the ground ahead.

He was unconscious when she reached him, blood from his head and . . . God, where else? . . . oozing into the mud around him. His cudgel lay beside him, and Kate grabbed it up, only to find that the deer were halted now, eyeing her silently like unholy demons.

Far in the distance she could see the running figures of Robyn and the other men, but she knew it would be some time before they could negotiate the paddocks and gates to reach her, and by then the stag herd might become aggressive again.

She turned, staring wildly around her. The gate! She was near a paddock boundary, a T-junction with the transit corridor, there should be one.

There! Only a few yards behind her. But what was in that paddock? She tried to remember, her mind fluttering over the many times she had walked this corridor. Fallow deer . . . she was sure of it. A mixed herd, but with the fallow not yet in the frenzy of their rut, there could be no danger.

Stooping, she tried to find a way of dragging Ben, but he was so heavy . . . her hands slipped off the slick oilskin when she grabbed at it. Finally she simply clamped her fingers into the collar of the coat, and felt nails breaking as his weight forced the material over them.

But he was moving! Sliding slowly but as if on some kind of sled, the slickness of the material now to her advantage on the wet ground.

Inch by inch she backed towards the gate, and finally she reached it, fumbled it open, reached down to grab at Ben's coat again. Heavens, but he was heavy! Dead weight.

Kate's mind screamed at the thought. No! Not dead. He couldn't be dead. She pulled harder, got most of him through the opening and ran to shift his legs aside and tug the gate closed again.

Safe! She flung herself down beside the still, white-faced figure, tearing away half the front of her shirt so that she had something with which to sponge away at the mud and blood that seemed to smother Ben.

Her ablutions only seemed to make matters worse, revealing a broad slash across his forehead and—worse—a deep cut near his crown that wouldn't stop bleeding no matter what she did.

'Oh, Ben, please don't die! Please, my love,' she whimpered, dabbing away at the gash that seemed to fill with blood as quickly as she removed it.

She ignored his other wounds. He could have a broken leg, or arms, for all Kate knew. All her attention was centred on that horrid, oozing wound from which it seemed his life was seeping on to the muddy ground.

She gently lifted his head, cradling it in her lap as she looked wildly about her. Where was everyone? Panic thrust up into her throat, a scream that wouldn't come to life as she choked it back.

'Oh God, oh please, Ben, don't die ... don't die ... don't die ...' she moaned over and over, babbling out the plea and then interspersing it with outpourings of her love for him, her true feelings, her soul.

And then, finally, her father was there with her, and Robyn. But it was a different Robyn from the one Kate was used to, a grim-faced woman who flatly told Henry to get his daughter away and bent to examine Ben with professional skill.

'It's all right, Kate. Calm down . . . calm down! Bill's gone for the truck and he'll be here in just a minute. We'll have him to the hospital before you know it,' her father soothed.

And then, miraculously, the truck was there, and Bill and Ken Lee were easing Ben on to a makeshift stretcher so they could lift him into the rear of the machine.

Kate flung herself free of her father's arms, springing up into the back of the Range Rover to cradle Ben's head as she had on the ground. Cradling him, protecting him, loving him.

But it was Robyn who took charge. Robyn, issuing orders like a regimental sergeant-major.

'Bill—you drive. Henry, go with him; you know the road. Ken, go and get your silly damned sister and take her back to the house; they'll drop me off as they pass the yards and I'll meet you there. Kate, you be careful of him. I think he's badly concussed and if he hasn't a few ribs broken I'll be surprised.'

And the truck doors were slamming shut and Bill was easing the machine carefully over the bumpy, rutted paddock, having to use four-wheel-drive to maintain any headway at all.

The drive was a nightmare. The truck slithered and slid and crept along over the treacherous road until Kate wanted to scream at Bill to hurry. Ben—her Ben—was dying. Her lap was awash with blood, her clothing splattered with it, her hands red.

And Ben was so . . . so white. His face was like chalk.

But he was breathing; his heart was beating.

It took a century to reach the bitumen, the blessed, rain-washed road surface that allowed Bill to push the heavy vehicle to its limits and beyond.

Another century, despite the increased speed, before they made it to Nambour and the hospital, to where trained medical staff could take charge, putting Ben on to a proper stretcher, and then wheeling him immediately away for treatment.

At that point Kate would have collapsed but for a kindly nursing aide who took her to where she could wash the blood from her hands, and try and clean up the rest of her as best she could.

As she stared into the mirror of the hospital washroom, the person staring back was a stranger, a wild-eyed, lank-haired stranger with a smudge of mud on one cheek and a face taut with emotional tensions.

The aide suggested she clean up; Kate said it wasn't important. The aide suggested it would do Ben no good at all to see Kate looking this way, so Kate cleaned up, helped by able, skilled hands, hands used to dealing with disaster.

There was nothing she could do about her shirt. Half the front was ripped away and the rest stained with blood—Ben's blood. Her jeans were even more badly stained. Only the cheap raincoat she had been wearing seemed immune from damage.

Kate did the best she could, then returned to the waiting room where Bill and her father had shed dripping oilskins and were sitting out their vigil with maddening patience.

Kate couldn't manage anything like it. She paced, sat down, paced some more. Her ears were alert to every step in the hospital corridors, every move by every white-coated attendant.

Each time anybody approached, she became instantly

alert, hoping this one would bring the good news. Or would it be good? Could Ben be dying, or maimed?

By the time an older, kindly-featured doctor finally did approach, Kate was almost past comprehending his words. It was Henry Lyle to whom he spoke.

'It isn't too serious. Some pretty bad cuts, a couple of cracked ribs. And he's concussed; I'm not too sure yet how badly. We'll have to keep him here a few days just for safety's sake. He can probably have visitors, oh . . . not tomorrow. Say the next day.'

Kate sagged at the knees with relief, would have fallen but for Bill's quick movement to catch her. He was all right! Suddenly the world swam before her eyes, swinging like a pendulum that grew swifter and swifter. Bill eased her down into a seat and the doctor rushed to her side. He probed and examined her briefly, then turned to her father.

'Just shock. I'll give you a sedative for her, but save it until you're home, if you can. She'll sleep a fair while.'

The voice seemed to fade into the roaring in her ears, but she heard him continue, 'Is this . . . Kim?'

Her father's reply was indistinct, but she heard the doctor yet again. '. . . just that he's been raving about somebody named Kim . . .'

CHAPTER NINE

KIM! The word echoed through the room, thundering like a cannon in Kate's ears. She flinched, huddling into herself, withdrawing from the sound.

Kim! Kate's soul shattered, tinkling around her like

brittle, sharded glass to leave only a vast, yawning chasm inside her, an emptiness not even her tears could fill. And cold . . . so horribly, deathly cold.

They wrapped her up for the journey home, using a car rug and her father's no-longer-needed oilskin. But she shivered, huddling mutely in his arms throughout the journey. The sun came out as they drove, but she only vaguely noticed. It could not warm her.

Back at Kathryn Downs, Robyn took charge. She forced Kate into a steaming, almost scalding shower. She forced her to swallow a quantity of steaming soup. She finally forced the sedative down her throat and helped her into bed, then piled on blankets and quilts. Kate merely shivered . . . and eventually slept.

When she woke it was dark and her body was warm again, but the chasm inside her was cold as ever, empty as the pit, and frightening.

Robyn was there. Dear Robyn. Robyn who examined her cautiously, then demanded she drink some warm tea, take another pill, and tucked her in again. This time she slept until morning, but she was still cold inside when she woke.

Her father was concerned at her appearance, her un-usual listlessness. Robyn declared it to be shock, and made her sit and listen while they telephoned the hospital.

Ben was resting comfortably. The concussion was less serious than they had feared. He could definitely have visitors tomorrow.

Kate listened, nodded, heard. He would be all right . . . for Kim. Damn Kim! But Kate damned her not from anger, but from sorrow; it was an ineffectual exercise. And if Ben Croft, *her* Ben, would be happier with his exotic Oriental beauty, so be it. So long as he was happy, and would in time be healthy again, Kate's own situation wasn't important.

Even when the Lees came to bid their farewells, imply-
ing without saying it outright that Kim wanted to be in
Nambour, so as to be close to Ben, Kate merely went
through the motions of saying goodbye, her mind and
heart numb, her lips uttering the expected platitudes without conscious thought.

At lunch, she fiddled with her food, not hungry but
equally unprepared to argue her lack of hunger with
anyone. Finally she ate just enough to forestall comment.
Then she pleaded a return of the chills and went to bed.

She came down to dinner, not bothering to dress but
wearing only her warmest housecoat and slippers, ate what
was put in front of her without tasting it, and went back to
bed.

And she slept; her numbed mind forced its will upon her
body, demanding sleep as the only escape from the turmoil
of emotions that whirled through the emptiness inside her
without touching, without gaining sufficient foothold to
make themselves live.

The next morning she woke early, but without her usual
thrill to the wild laughter of the kookaburras and the gentle
gabbling of Robyn's geese. Today, she thought, Ben could
have visitors. And she could not ... must not ... allow
herself to be forced into going. She couldn't!

Throwing on her most worn clothing, she started off to
make her habitual morning patrol of the paddocks, but
too many memories lay within the sparkling, dew-
drenched grasses, too much of Ben was there. When Bill
sauntered out to join her, having already done half the
patrol before Kate had begun, she was glad for his silence,
his unquestioning acceptance of her decision to cut short
the walk that morning.

He went on without her, and she didn't look back. Not

even when she passed the site of Ben's accident, the spot where she had cradled his head and poured out her heart in a prayer for his safety.

They came for her just before lunch, as she had known they would. Everyone was going in; they would have lunch in town and then visit Ben, make an afternoon of it.

Kate declined, her mind a whirlwind of vague excuses before an unexpected sniffle gave her a valid one. A cold! Perfect. And if not perfect, at least sufficient to allow her to beg off.

'It would be silly for me to go,' she said. 'I mean, the last thing he needs is me passing on my germs.'

Robyn looked at her sceptically, opened her mouth as if to argue, then snapped it shut again. When she finally spoke there was a lightness in her tone.

'Perhaps you're right, Kate. Shall I give him your love, then?'

Damn you, Robyn! Innocent words that slice like a razor, if they're really innocent. 'Give him my regards, certainly,' Kate replied with astonishing calm.

Once they were gone, she cooked herself a simple but filling meal, then studiously cleaned up the evidence of it. When they returned she fled to her bedroom, feigning sleep like a child trying to escape punishment.

But she heard their voices, knew that Ben was recovering, that there would be no complications. Something inside her felt intense pleasure from that; most of her remained deliberately numb. When Robyn came to see if she would like dinner, Kate again pretended to be asleep, hiding her head beneath the covers. She remembered that a person pretending sleep could always be discovered by the flickering of their eyelids.

In the morning she went down for breakfast looking weary and wan despite all the rest she appeared to have had. She, of course, knew better. Her mind was forcing sleep on a body that didn't need it; she felt wooden, stiff. Her mind worked, but only just.

Fortunately, no one else appeared much brighter and for once even Robyn seemed averse to the usual idle breakfast chatter. They all ate, drank their coffee, and then dispersed to whatever chores awaited. Kate had none.

The best part of breakfast was the decision to wait until tomorrow to visit Ben again. When Kate could come with them, her cold no longer a hindrance.

She nodded agreement without meaning it, unable to readily concoct a suitable excuse for not going. She would think of one during the day, somehow. She'd have to . . . the thought of having to visit with Ben in a hospital room, of having to share her time with him, watch him and Kim exchanging affectionate greetings — it wasn't to be contemplated.

Here, on her own ground, she could perhaps manage to face him. Somehow. At least she would have time to prepare; he would undoubtedly return to his Brisbane home, where Kim could assist in his convalescence, before coming back here.

Kate spent most of the day indoors, pretending to read but in reality only wallowing in a growing morass of self-pity and self-doubt. She didn't see the words on the pages she turned; she saw herself, saw once again the horrible nagging guilt of wishing a husband dead, and of finally, truly, loving—only to have that love lost, wasted. Perhaps, she thought, it was only just. A proper retribution for her earlier sorceries.

It didn't matter, really. She obviously couldn't carry on like this. Robyn was showing signs of growing impatience with her moodiness; her father soon would, as well.

Kate finished her breakfast next morning with still no idea how she would get out of having to visit Ben that day, and she was elbow-deep in dishwater afterwards when Robyn brought up the subject without warning.

'I suppose you'll want to stay home again today,' she said without preamble. 'Have you thought up an excuse yet?'

Kate was stunned, as much by the bluntness of the question as by what was actually said. 'I . . . er . . . I . . . don't know,' she finally stammered.

'Yes, there's a lot you don't know,' Robyn sneered. 'You're obviously going to have to face him sooner or later, or haven't you thought that far ahead yet?'

'Not . . . really, no,' said Kate.

'Naturally. But of course this is all because you're madly in love with him, and he doesn't love you, and you'll just die with the trauma of it all,' Robyn continued, her voice dripping with sarcasm. 'Kate, you're a weep. Worse than a weep—you're acting like a fifteen-year-old schoolgirl. Lord! I don't know how you could expect to even *attract* a man like Ben with that kind of childish outlook, much less hook him for good. He's a man, not a child.

'Now I have to say this, for your own good. I don't much like it and you'll probably hate me, but damn it, somebody's got to. Grow up! *Grow . . . up!* You can't live in the past; you can't blame Ben for the bastard your first husband was; and you can't live the rest of your life with this idiotic guilt.'

Kate stood there, mouth open in astonishment at the harshness of Robyn's criticism. 'But . . . but . . .' she floundered over the words.

'But nothing! You're twenty-six years old and you've been moping around here for days like a two-year-old with hurt feelings. I'm sick of it; your father's sick of it; and if

Ben were here he'd be sickened *by* it,' Robyn snapped. 'Now for God's sake get your head together before I really lose my temper and give you the licking you deserve!'

It was the sheer vehemence of the assault that got through to Kate where a softer line wouldn't have. It seemed as if she'd been slapped across the face, and the slap cracked the façade and let reality in with a rush of embarrassment.

She stood there, meeting Robyn's eyes with her own, for a long moment. Then, 'You're right, of course,' she said very quietly. 'And I really do apologise. It's just that . . .'

'It's just that it hurts a lot and hiding seemed the easiest way out,' Robyn said gently. 'I know, Kate. I've been there a time or two myself. But all you can do is put on your best public face and keep on going, believe me. Especially under circumstances like these, where there are so many people involved who honestly care for you both.'

Kate smiled wanly. 'Yes,' she said, 'all right.'

'Good. Then we won't talk about it any more,' Robyn said. 'Instead we'll talk about the menu for his "coming out" party and just hope it doesn't take too much longer. We should find out today, with any luck.'

Two hours later, Kate was in her room trying to decide what to wear when she heard the phone ring, and a few minutes later Robyn knocked at her door.

'Looks like you get a reprieve,' she said. 'That was Ben. Seems they're going to let him out today, but something's come up in Brisbane, so Ken Lee's going to drive him straight there. He said he didn't have time to explain, but I guess we'll have to postpone our little celebration dinner until he comes back.'

'I can just imagine what's come up in Brisbane,' Kate replied, trying to keep her voice light. But she couldn't bring herself to say the rest. Kim Lee! And Robyn, fortunately, didn't ask her to elaborate.

'Well, I can't say I'm all that upset, since he's all right now anyway,' said Robyn. 'It seems as if all I've been doing lately is cook fancy-dancy meals. Tonight I think I'll stay home and gorge on plain old spaghetti, and if Bill doesn't like it, he can complain to the management. In fact, I think we should let him and your father fend for themselves just for a change; it's not as if they were helpless. You can come over and share my spaghetti, if you like.'

'Don't you think it would make more sense to share it with Dad, while I stay here and cook for Bill as usual?' said Kate. 'It can't be much fun sharing your romance with a bachelor brother and a half-witted daughter all the time.'

'We're managing just fine, thank you,' Robyn retorted, 'although that's not a bad idea. I'll think about it.'

But at lunch it developed that Bill had other ideas. There was a movie he wanted to see in town, so he'd go in early and pick up something to eat in the pub. Henry Lyle was delighted to share the spaghetti in the company of his fiancée, and Kate secretly thought neither he nor Robyn was too upset when she volunteered to leave them to it and subsist on her own cooking for a change.

After cleaning up, she looked out at the brilliance of the sunshine and decided that it was too nice a day for work of any kind. Instead, she would walk up to her pool and see if it had subsided enough after the heavy rains to allow her an afternoon of swimming and sunbathing.

Her confrontation with Robyn seemed to have cleared away the cobwebs from her mind, and although she was still deeply hurt at losing Ben to Kim Lee, she now felt able to cope. It wouldn't be easy, Kate thought, but neither would it be impossible.

The path to her pool was still boggy in places, but she

was delighted to find the upper reaches of the stream
running bank-full but clean; even the platypus was out
enjoying the sunshine, and she paused for a moment to
watch him before hurrying on to her pool.

Her pool! As always it was a place of supreme solitude,
with the tumbling waters and muted greens of the surrounding bush combining to make it a haven of peace.

Quickly, she stripped away her clothing, unbound her
hair and flung herself into the chilly water, swimming up
and down and across the pool in a furious bid to keep
warm. When she was tired, she lifted herself up on to her
rock and lay back to let the sun warm her, feeling the heat
soak into her body as if it were a sponge.

There was something about the solitude of the place,
the somnolent heat of the sun on the rocks. She swam and
sunbathed and swam again, then slipped out on to the
rock for a final lazy bake before heading back.

'That looks very pleasant. Perhaps I should join you.'

Ben's words drawled across the water, and Kate gave no
thought whatsoever to the smart replies of her long-ago
fantasy. With a shriek of surprise and embarrassment she
rolled off the far side of the rock and into the relative
sanctuary of the water.

'Oh, did I frighten you? Sorry about that,' he said, his
lips quirked into a smile that showed he wasn't one bit
sorry.

'Will you get out of here!' Kate demanded. Then, even
in her shock and surprise, she found herself wondering
how he'd got there in the first place. A broad white bandage was cocked raffishly around his head, and from the
way he was leaning on a long walking staff, he seemed to
be in some pain.

'Oh,' she exclaimed. 'Are you all right?'

'It only hurts when I laugh,' he growled, 'but I haven't

been doing much of that, lately.'

Wincing slightly with the effort, he slowly lowered himself until he was sitting on a large rock near the water's edge.

'You're going to get cold if you stay there too long,' he said. 'Why don't you get back on your rock where it's warm?'

'You know very well why,' Kate retorted. 'What are you *doing* here?'

'Well, I was looking at you. And rather enjoying it, too, I might say. Splendid medicine for a convalescent. Why don't you climb up there again? Or don't you like me looking at you?'

'I certainly do not,' she lied, glad that the rock hid her from his gaze. Not because of her nudity, but because she couldn't help the purely physical reaction her body displayed to his visual caresses.

'Ah well, you've got to come out some time. I've got plenty of time,' he said, fumbling in his shirt pocket until he had found a cigarette and lit it. 'Want one?'

'I'd rather have my clothes—and my privacy,' she replied.

'Sorry, I'm only offering cigarettes at the moment,' he grinned. 'I could bring it out to you . . .'

'You'll do no such thing,' Kate snapped. 'You're supposed to be in hospital. Are you quite mad?'

'Probably. I think it's the concussion; I keep hearing voices.'

Voices! Kate shivered, but it wasn't from the water. What was he doing out of the hospital if he was hearing voices?

'You should be in bed,' she charged.

'Boring. Nobody to talk to, nothing to do.'

'I think that kick in the head did more damage than

you realise,' she replied. 'Did you walk all the way up here from the house?'

'Of course not. Do you think I'm daft?' he replied. 'I brought the Range Rover most of the way.'

'But ... why?' she fumed, scowling at him from her shelter.

'Oh, maybe I thought I'd catch a water nymph sunbathing on a rock,' he replied. 'Very good medicine, water nymphs. Or,' and his voice lowered suggestively, 'maybe I fancied a swim. Shall I join you?'

'Don't you dare!' Kate's concern now was not for herself, but for him. Obviously he was deranged; only an idiot would climb into that chill water after what he'd been through.

He shrugged. 'Well then, get back on the rock. I find it disturbing having to try and converse with a floating head.'

'Don't be ludicrous,' she said crossly.

'Ah, well,' He stood up, slowly and carefully, and began unbuttoning his shirt. Beneath it Kate could see the tape that was wrapped around his rib cage. Cracked ribs, the doctor had said ...

'Don't!' she shrieked. 'You can't come in here; you'll get your bandages all wet.'

'Well then, come out.' His face was non-revealing, but his eyes laughed at her, mocking her.

'No!'

'What are you afraid of? Surely not a man with a banged-up head and half his ribs cracked?'

'I'm afraid you'll hurt yourself, you silly fool,' she cried angrily.

'Humph! If you were really worried about me you'd have come to see me at the hospital,' he said, continuing to open up the shirt.

'I . . . couldn't,' she replied. 'I had a cold. Will you *stop* that!'

'I don't believe you. If you had a cold you're an even bigger fool than I am, puddling about in water that cool.'

'Well, I wouldn't be if you'd just get out of here so I could get dressed,' she shouted.

'Nice and warm on that rock, in the sun,' he replied with a grin. 'Think of it as therapy for a sick man.'

'You're sick all right,' Kate muttered. And thought, Oh, Ben, don't you know how you're torturing me?

'What was that?'

'I didn't say anything.'

'No, but you thought it; I could see the wheels going round. Now tell me.'

'I won't!'

'Oh yes, you will,' he said, lean fingers reaching now for the buckle of his belt.

'You stop that!' she squealed. 'Are you utterly mad?'

'I don't see what's so mad about wanting to sport awhile with a water nymph,' he chuckled. 'It's not often one gets the chance.'

'I am not a water nymph,' she retorted. 'And you are *not* coming in here. You'll do yourself an injury!'

'I really don't know why you're being so stubborn,' he replied. 'If you don't want me getting my bandages wet then all you have to do is climb out on the rock where I can see you.'

'That's . . . that's blackmail!' Kate snapped.

'Yup!' He sat down again and began pulling at his boots, wincing with pain every time he leaned down to tug at them. Clearly his cracked ribs weren't up to this kind of activity.

'Ben! Stop it!' she cried. 'Oh, damn you anyway. You don't care what harm you do yourself, so long as you get your own way.'

'Ah, now you're getting the picture,' he grinned, then changed the grin for a slight grimace of pain as he straightened up again.

'Oh . . . Ben, please . . .' she pleaded.

'You still haven't told me what you were thinking,' he replied. His boots were off now, and he was struggling to wriggle his socks off with his toes to keep from having to bend over again.

'I was thinking you've freaked out entirely,' she lied. 'What did they give you at that hospital, anyway . . . some kind of happy pills?'

'Don't lie to me,' he said, and Kate felt the touch of whiplash in his voice for the first time. 'You've lied to me too damned often as it is, and I'll have no more of it.'

'I have *not*!' Kate hoped she had enough indignation in her voice to fool him into believing her.

'See . . . you're doing it again. Damn it, woman, you must like playing with fire,' he said. 'You try and convince me you're a conventional grieving widow when you're not, you try and convince me you're not interested in me when you are . . . I suppose next you'll be trying to tell me you don't love me, either.'

'My God, but you're an egotist!' Kate exclaimed, turning her eyes away. Somehow she had to turn this conversation to another subject, she thought, or she'd be undone for certain. 'And I didn't lie to you either,' she said with a rush. 'I was . . . grieving and I never . . . never denied a physical attraction between us.'

'Like hell! If you were grieving at all it was for yourself, not that rotten bastard you were married to,' he replied. 'Damn it anyway; I wish he was still alive, sometimes, so I could kill him myself—by inches. I've never seen such an outright case of ego-destruction as that . . . that . . . as he worked on you. And you still won't even admit it, which is worse yet.'

'Oh, I admit it all right,' Kate snapped. 'Oh yes, I admit it. But I don't see that you've got any right to complain; at least Wayne had the decency, if you can call it that, to marry me before he started trying to run my life. All you've done is try to take advantage of me, as if I was some sort of convenience that goes with the farm.'

'The hell I have! What in blazes are you talking about?' Ben demanded.

'You know very well what I'm talking about,' Kate shrilled. 'And if you think I'm going to spell it out chapter and verse just to boost your puny little ego some more, then think again!'

'There's nothing puny about my ego,' he retorted. 'It's a very healthy, active and energetic ego, usually. Except when I'm dealing with a woman who won't talk sense and won't do anything but lie to me without even a good reason.'

'I'm not lying to you,' she cried, more than half angry now.

'Well then, why won't you admit you love me? Are you afraid to admit it—even to yourself?'

Kate peered suspiciously at him while she thought desperately for a solution. Damn him anyway, she thought. Did he really intend to humiliate her by forcing an answer?

'If I admit it will you let me get out of here and get dressed?' she asked. 'I really am getting chilly.'

'I'll think about it.' His bland expression couldn't mask the triumph in those hateful green eyes.

'Well, think about it until you're blue in the face,' she snapped angrily. 'I'll freeze to death in here before I'll allow you to humiliate me into such a stupid admission.

You can just go straight to hell, Ben Croft!'

'All right, I will!' he shouted back at her, rising quickly to his feet. But then, to Kate's horror, he gasped and slumped to sprawl flat on his back beside the rock where he had been sitting.

'Ben! Oh, my God . . . Ben!' she screamed, and when he didn't move immediately she flashed round her rock and streaked for the shore. She clambered out, oblivious of the shards of rock beneath her feet, and ran to kneel beside him, her eyes brimming with tears.

One hand went out to touch his forehead, which seemed frighteningly pale, and the other went down to lift his wrist so she could check his pulse.

'Oh, Ben,' she whispered, a whisper that turned to a moan and then a cry of surprise as his fingers closed round her wrist and his other arm flew up to clasp itself round her waist and pull her down against him.

His lips claimed her with savage persistence, giving her no chance to pull away, no chance to fight. And she was lost . . . betrayed by heart and soul and body as she felt the heat of his bare chest against her breasts, the thrilling touch of his fingers at the small of her back.

He rolled sideways enough that her weight was off his taped rib-cage, but his lips never gave up their onslaught on her passion-softened mouth, and his free hand continued its gentle, persuasive caresses.

Kate squirmed, not trying to free herself now, but snuggling closer to him, moulding her body with his, her lips moving as she returned his kiss. She wriggled her hand free and slipped it around his neck, fingers groping for the hair at his nape as she returned his caresses ardently.

She felt his hand slide down, lightly touching her cheek, her throat, then cupping her breast for an endless moment before it slid down across the tautness of her stomach, each touch further rousing her, further wakening her to the delights of his touch.

He bent to kiss her breast, and she felt his groan of pain as much as heard it.

'Damn,' he muttered, 'maybe I did leave the hospital too soon.'

'You're hurt!'

'No, but I will be if this goes on much longer,' he whispered. 'Just as well anyway; I wouldn't want to compromise you.'

'Well, I don't know what else you could call it,' she whispered back, then stifled a giggle. 'And you were shamming, you devil!'

'It worked, didn't it? That's what counts. It got you over here where I could talk to you by hand, which seems to be much more effective than shouting over the water.'

'Too effective. Let me up,' she replied. But his fingers flashed up to grasp her wrist before she could move.

'Not without some answers, my dear Kate,' he said. 'True ones, this time. Are you going to admit you love me, or do I have to risk my ribs again and force it out of you?'

'I would say the answer's pretty obvious,' she hedged, a simple yes on the tip of her tongue, but some perverse demon stopping her from saying it.

'You said it better on the way to the hospital,' he urged, leaning up to kiss her lightly on the mouth.

'You . . . you heard?'

'Umm. Some of it, anyway. But I thought I must be dreaming, especially when you wouldn't come to visit me. *Why* wouldn't you, Kate?'

Why? Why indeed? she thought. 'Because . . . because I thought you . . . wanted somebody else,' she admitted. 'You were . . . I heard the doctor say you were raving for . . . for . . .'

'For Kim. Ah, that's it! Well, I was, too. Damned silly woman nearly got you killed, and I'd have broken her neck if I could have got my hands on her.'

'But . . . but I thought . . . Wasn't she visiting you in the hospital? When they left here it was to . . .'

'Oh, she visited me all right. She stuck her nose in the door and nearly got a water carafe bounced off it,' he laughed. 'Probably half the reason my ribs are so tender; they don't react kindly to such treatment.'

He grinned at her, then, eyes no longer mocking, but filled with compassion, tenderness.

'Poor dear Kate,' he murmured. 'You were jealous of her after all, weren't you? I didn't think you would be, although I tried hard enough to make sure you were.'

'But . . . but why? You don't . . . couldn't . . .' Kate couldn't get the words out, but Ben had no such problem.

'Love you?' he asked softly. 'Well, of course I love you, you silly woman. I loved you even before you got here.'

Part of her mind heard him, couldn't believe. Another part thrilled so she could hardly speak.

'But . . . but that's impossible,' she gasped, her objection hampered considerably by what he was doing with his free hand.

'No, it's not. I fell in love, dear Kate, with your picture. Or pictures . . . your father has quite a few, and one way or another I made sure he showed me every one of them. Even,' and he kissed her lightly on the nose, 'the one of you naked on the sheepskin rug when you were about one year old. Very fetching, although I like you better this way.'

'Oh, Ben . . . stop that! I can't concentrate on what you're saying,' Kate whispered, her body writhing in ecstasy at his touch.

'Just think of it as wordless communication,' he

murmured, lips closing on hers with slow, infinite, knowing skill. And then, 'Oh, hell! You'd better get dressed, I suppose. My poor old ribs won't stand up to what's liable to happen if you don't.'

'Typical masculine approach,' she giggled. 'You complain and scheme until you get what you want, and then claim you can't handle it.'

'Well, it's better than pretending to have a headache, wench . . . and at least I can get a doctor's certificate,' he laughed in reply, slapping her soundly on the haunch. 'Now get a move on, before I forget my good intentions.'

He flung himself over on his back, cradling his head on one arm and closing his eyes against the glare of the high, bright sun.

'See, I won't even look,' he said. 'Provided of course that you hurry; I'm only human, after all.'

Kate, busy scrambling into her jeans and shirt, could barely manage to restrain a whoop of sheer delight. He was only human. And he loved her. Her! Not Kim Lee, not anyone else. Her! It was incredible, unbelievable.

She turned to him when she was clothed, suddenly shy for whatever ludicrous sense that made. 'Did you really only use Kim to make me jealous, or . . .'

'Or was there really something between us? No, darling Kate, there wasn't. Never was and never would be, although I now feel that Kim might have thought differently. I've known her for years, through her brother, and I've always sort of teased her along, but never more than that. She's lovely—even you can't deny that—but she's the most self-centred little bitch I've ever run across. I wouldn't even have dared get "involved" with her, to put it politely, because I'm far too cautious by nature for that kind of risk.'

'You . . . cautious? I don't believe that,' said Kate,

kneeling to snuggle against him again, lips brushing against his ear.

'Well, of course I'm cautious,' he said. 'And let me tell you, *you* had me pretty worried for a while. You didn't seem anything like the girl your father had described to me so often. I didn't know what to make of you.'

'I think I can understand that, now,' Kate replied gently. 'I was really very, very mixed up. And very, very defensive.'

'Defensive isn't the word for it. I couldn't figure out whether you were really grieving, which I couldn't quite understand from what your father said about ... oh, whatever his name was. Then I thought that maybe you'd really been terribly in love with him despite him being such a proper swine, and I didn't know how to proceed if that were true.'

'No, I wasn't in love with him. Now I realise I never was,' Kate replied soberly. 'Just infatuated, at least in the beginning. Thinking back, I'm not sure why I even stayed with him ... it would have been totally self-destructive if he ... if he hadn't died.'

'Died on his way home from the arms of a scrubby little tart,' Ben muttered angrily. 'And to have it come out during the inquest, as of course it had to, that must have been hell for you.'

'You really did do a lot of checking, didn't you?' Kate replied. 'I'm still not sure I like that.'

'I had to,' he replied. 'It was obvious something was the matter with you, and *you* obviously weren't going to en-lighten me. Like I said, I'm a cautious person. And I wanted to know, so I damned well made sure I found out.'

'You didn't find out everything, you know,' she said, rolling away so that she was out of his arms, but still touching him, still able to look at him.

'Oh?' The question was there, but he didn't say another word. No pushing, no prodding, only a look in those patient green eyes.

Kate swallowed. It was hard to begin, but once started she blurted it out, everything.

'The . . . the night Wayne died, was killed, I was . . . I was sitting at home and wishing he would die,' she said. 'Yes, actually sitting there and wishing him dead. I was still doing it when the . . . the police came, and when they told me, I . . . I just felt so horribly guilty. I know, I knew then that the wishing was only a defence mechanism, that it didn't really mean I wanted him . . . *dead*. But he was. And it was as if I'd . . . killed him.'

Then she was in Ben's arms, sobbing against the crisp hair on his chest as his arms wrapped protectively around her, holding her, cherishing her.

She was there for ever, it seemed, drenching them both in a flood of tears she couldn't stop. But he said nothing, only held her and stroked her, gentling her and soothing her with his touch.

'I'm . . . sorry,' she blubbered finally. And then, 'No, no, I'm not. I needed to get it out, to say it. It was just that, living with Wayne, the way he was, I think it really disrupted my own self-image. He was weak, really, but oh, so domineering, and so skilled at manipulating people, hurting people. Hurting me. I really thought our marriage going sour was all my fault.'

'And was it?'

'Not entirely, but I know now that I contributed a great deal by letting him dominate me so badly. Not that I think it would have saved the marriage if I hadn't, but it was definitely a factor. Oh, Ben, don't you see that it was exactly because of that . . . the domination thing . . . that I was so afraid to let you get too close. I was afraid ... really afraid.'

'I presume that was before you realised I wasn't quite the same type as your former husband,' he said drily.

'I always knew you weren't the same type, silly,' Kate retorted, gulping. 'Right from the very first time I met you, when you cooked for me, and put me to bed like a good little girl. But you're strong ... so very strong.'

'Damned good thing, too, or you'd have got away,' he chuckled. 'But too late now, my love. Far too late. Now that I've got you, I'm going to keep you right under my thumb, just like an old stag with his harem.'

'I'd rather like that,' Kate grinned back. 'But only if it means I get to be the whole harem, all by myself. I don't think I'd enjoy sharing you.'

'You won't have to,' Ben assured her. 'Not even on your wedding day, just in case you've got any silly ideas about a double wedding. I believe in doing one thing at a time and doing it well, so first we'll get your father and Robyn married off. I mean, they can't afford any delays at their age.'

'And we can? Not if you keep up with this kind of thing,' Kate laughed, reaching down to brush his tantalising fingers from her breast.

Ben merely replaced them with his lips, stifling a wince as the bending action pulled at his tender ribs. Then he lay back, green eyes laughing up at her.

'We'll have to,' he said, reaching down to prod angrily at the tape and then less harshly at the bandage across his forehead. 'I'd look damned silly in wedding photos with this bandage on, and these cracked ribs might ... inhibit me in other, more important ways.'

'Oh, I don't know,' Kate laughed. 'I could always say I'd cut off your horns for their velvet; that would explain the bandage.'

'Don't be cheeky,' he growled in mock fierceness. Rolling away from her, he eased himself gingerly to his feet, then attempted futilely to reach down and lift her as well.

She shook her head at his wince of pain, and stood upright without the assistance.

'Maybe I won't marry you after all,' she said teasingly. 'It's obvious you're just a decrepit old man. You probably drink antler velvet tea every morning just to get the strength to get out of bed.'

Ben laughed, his eyes deep green pools of love. 'I'll arrange some for our wedding dinner,' he promised gravely. 'Just to see if it works.'

'Somehow,' said Kate, 'I don't think you'll need it.'

HARLEQUIN
PREMIERE AUTHOR EDITIONS

6 EXCITING HARLEQUIN AUTHORS
—6 OF THEIR BEST BOOKS!

Daphne Clair
A STREAK OF GOLD

Marjorie Lewty
TO CATCH A BUTTERFLY

Anne Mather
SCORPIONS' DANCE

Jessica Steele
SPRING GIRL

Margaret Way
THE WILD SWAN

Violet Winspear
DESIRE HAS NO MERCY

Harlequin is pleased to offer these six very special titles, out of print since 1980. These authors have published over 250 titles between them. Popular demand required that we reissue each of these exciting romances in new beautifully designed covers.

Available in April wherever paperback books are sold, or through Harlequin Reader Service. Simply send your name, address and zip or postal code, with a check or money order for $2.50 for each copy ordered (includes 75¢ for postage and handling) payable to Harlequin Reader Service, to:

Harlequin Reader Service

In the U.S.
P.O. Box 52040
Phoenix, AZ 85072-2040

In Canada
P.O. Box 2800
Postal Station A
5170 Yonge Street
Willowdale, Ontario
M2N 6J3